A DONUT SHOP MYSTERY

# EVIL ÉCLAIRS

## JESSICA BECK

WHEELER
CHIVERS

This Large Print edition is published by Wheeler Publishing, Waterville, Maine, USA and by AudioGO Ltd, Bath, England.
Wheeler Publishing, a part of Gale, Cengage Learning.

**ALL RIGHTS RESERVED**

Wheeler Publishing Large Print Cozy Mystery.
The text of this Large Print edition is unabridged.
Other aspects of the book may vary from the original edition.
Set in 16 pt. Plantin.

**LIBRARY OF CONGRESS CATALOGING-IN-PUBLICATION DATA**

Beck, Jessica.
    Evil éclairs : a donut shop mystery / by Jessica Beck. — Large print ed.
        p. cm. — (Wheeler Publishing large print cozy mystery)
    ISBN-13: 978-1-4104-3813-3 (pbk.)
    ISBN-10: 1-4104-3813-9 (pbk.)
    1. Coffee shops—North Carolina—Fiction. 2. Private investigators—Fiction. 3. North Carolina—Fiction. 4. Large type books. I. Title.
    PS3602.E2693E85 2011
    813'.6—dc22                                        2011014100

BRITISH LIBRARY CATALOGUING-IN-PUBLICATION DATA AVAILABLE

Published in 2011 in the U.S. by arrangement with St. Martin's Press, LLC.
Published in 2011 in the U.K. by arrangement with the author.

U.K. Hardcover: 978 1 445 83818 2 (Chivers Large Print)
U.K. Softcover: 978 1 445 83819 9 (Camden Large Print)

Printed and bound in Great Britain by the MPG Books Group
1 2 3 4 5 6 7 15 14 13 12 11

# EVIL ÉCLAIRS

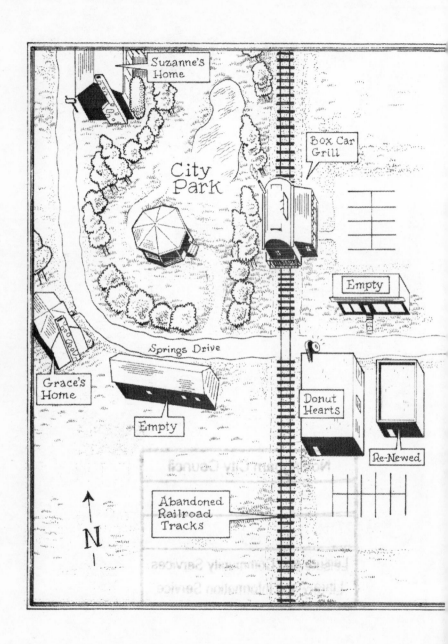

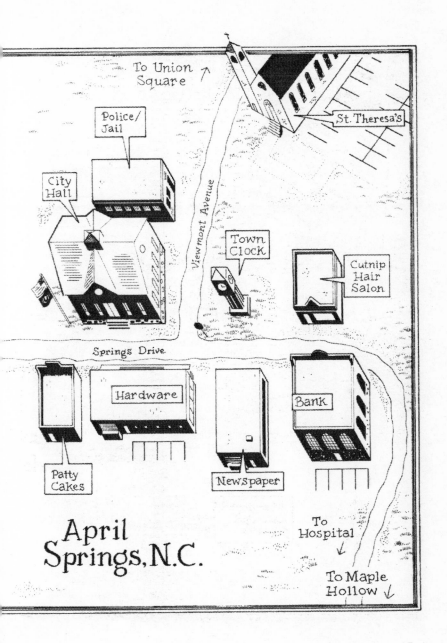

Between the optimist and pessimist, the difference is droll. The optimist sees the doughnut, the pessimist, the hole!

— Oscar Wilde

# CHAPTER 1

Owning and running a donut shop is not for the faint of heart. If I'm going to get anywhere close to the minimum six hours of sleep I need before I get up at one A.M. every morning, I have to be in bed by seven every night.

Tonight I'd pushed my bedtime back too far and I knew I'd pay for it in the morning. As I drifted off to sleep just after eight, I heard the name of my donut shop mentioned on the radio. That was odd, since I had never been able to afford even their low advertising rates to tout my specialty donut and coffee shop.

Then I realized that Donut Hearts wasn't being described with any affection. Lester Moorefield, the local news jockey on WAPS, was broadcasting another of his diatribes, and this time, I was evidently his target. His show ran in the morning, but his editorials were always done at night.

"Donuts are a perfect example of how we are slowly killing ourselves. To give you just one instance, I sat in my car across the street from Donut Hearts this morning, and in one hour, I saw countless overweight or downright obese people stumbling out of the place with glazed looks on their faces and powdered sugar on their lips. Suzanne Hart feeds this sickness within her customers, catering to their base cravings like some kind of dealer. Her products are toxic, deadly dough, if you will, and we in the community need to take a stand. I propose that over the next seven days, the citizens of April Springs, and all within the sound of my voice in North Carolina, boycott this shop, and others of its ilk, and stand up to those who would enslave us with their tempting but fatal offerings."

Suddenly I was wide awake.

Momma was sitting by the radio downstairs, and from the expression on her face, she hadn't missed a word of Lester's diatribe, either. I'd barely taken the time to throw on some sweatpants and an old T-shirt before I'd raced downstairs.

"That man is a menace to society," she said. "Someone should stop him." Though my mother was physically slight, barely five feet tall, she more than made up for it with her fierce spirit.

"He's gone too far this time," I agreed as I threw on my running shoes. I wouldn't win any Best Dressed awards for my ensemble, but I wasn't about to take time to consider my wardrobe.

"What are you doing?" Momma asked.

"Isn't it obvious?" I asked as I struggled with one shoelace that had somehow managed to knot itself into a mess. "I'm going to go see him at the station."

"Suzanne, don't do anything reckless."

"Why not?" I asked. I was about to get a knife to cut the lace's knot when it started to come loose of its own accord. "In a situation like this, sometimes that's exactly what's called for."

Momma stood and looked at me. "One thing I learned early on; you should never pick a fight with a lawyer or someone who has their own bully pulpit. I don't like it any more than you do, but if you leave Lester alone, tomorrow he'll move on to his next victim and you can go about your business."

There, the knot came free. "Momma, too many people roll over and play dead for that man. Well, not me. If he wants a fight, he's got one."

I grabbed my jacket as I started for the door. It was early April, and the weather could be chilly in the evening but still have a hint of real warmth in the middle of the day.

Momma stood and reached for her own coat.

I stopped in my tracks. "Where do you think you're going?"

"With you, of course," she said, clearly puzzled by the question.

"Momma, I love you with all my heart, but this is my battle, not yours."

I may have tweaked her a little with the declaration, but it had to be said. I'd given up a great deal of my independence when I'd moved back in with her after my divorce from Max, and I found myself reverting to old habits sometimes. But I had to do this by myself. I was a grown woman, able to fight my own wars.

Her jacket went back on the rack, and I found myself trying to soften the blow. "I don't mean to hurt your feelings, but I have to do this alone. You understand, don't you?"

"Suzanne, of course you're right. Sometimes I forget that you're not a child anymore."

"A small part of me will always be your

little girl. You know that, right?"

She looked pleased by my comment. "You should go now so you can catch him in the act. It's like housebreaking a puppy. If you don't point out the mistake to them right away, they'll never learn."

"I'll rub his nose in it, all right," I said with a grin. "Wish me luck."

She smiled at me. "I have a feeling it's Lester, not you, who will need the luck."

"I believe you're right."

I got into my Jeep and drove to the radio station on the outskirts of April Springs. As I started on my way across town, I passed Grace Gauge's place. Grace and I had grown up together, and she'd been my best friend just about my entire life. We'd stayed close, and the years had done nothing to loosen our bond.

And then I came to Donut Hearts. It was odd seeing my old converted train depot this time of night. I always felt a tug when I saw the place. I'd bought my shop almost as a whim on the heels of my divorce from Max, but it had been the best stroke of luck I've ever had in my life. The shop kept me busy, alive, and connected to the world around me. It also made it tough to feel sorry for myself after my marriage fell apart. In truth, I was just about too busy to notice.

15

I drove past the town clock, and soon enough, I saw the police station. I thought of Jake Bishop when I did. He was an investigator for the state police, and had recently added being my steady boyfriend to his résumé. We'd endured some rocky moments in our relationship from the start, but since the previous Christmas, we'd managed to overcome most of them. I knew that he'd done his best to get over his late wife, and I was glad that I'd been patient until he was ready to move on with his life.

Jake was turning out to be worth the wait, after all.

Soon enough, I was in the parking lot of our local radio station, WAPS. I'd feared for a moment that Lester had taped his editorial, since he had a live program he broadcast every morning, but luckily for me, his car was in the parking lot, along with another that had to belong to his producer. I'd never been a fan of Lester's, but I really liked Cara Lassiter. She'd helped me before when I'd had trouble with Lester, and I was in fact surprised she hadn't warned me about what was coming.

I knocked on the door, and I saw the TV camera above it swing around to me.

"Cara, it's Suzanne."

The door buzzed, and I walked into the

16

building.

She met me before I managed to get three paces inside. "Suzanne, I would have warned you about what he was doing, but I had no idea who he was skewering tonight. By the time I could have called you, it would have been too late to do anything about it, and he would have fired me in the bargain."

"I don't have a problem with you," I said. "Where is he?"

She looked around the small station. "I don't know; he was right here a second ago. He just signed off the air for the night."

I looked into the broadcasting booth, and then his small but neat office. It, too, was empty. "Where is he, then?"

"If I had to guess, I'd say that he's probably on his way out to grab a quick smoke."

I looked back the way I'd come. "I didn't see him go out."

"He uses the employee entrance. Suzanne, you can't win with him, you know that, don't you?"

"Maybe not, but I'm not just going to take it."

I started for the door. "Care to come with me? You can be a witness."

Cara grinned at me. "I'd love to, but if he knew I was watching you ream him out, he'd fire me for sure."

"I understand. Maybe you can watch on the security camera."

I went out the door, and sure enough, there was Lester, leaning against his car with a glowing cigarette in his hand. With the streetlight across the way, I could see him just fine. Lester was a tall and lean man, with a sharp nose and eyes that didn't miss much. His hair was greased back with some kind of product, and he wore a suit that hadn't been in style for years.

Why did he not look at all surprised to see me?

Of course, my Jeep was parked right there beside him.

I'd have given anything to wipe the smug look off his face. He said, "I was wondering if you heard my broadcast. What did you think?"

"You are a coward and a weasel, and I'm going to sue you for what little you must have for what you just said." I tried to keep my voice calm, but it was more than I could manage. At least I wasn't yelling. Not yet, anyway.

My words brought a smile to his face. "Take your best shot. I'm protected by the First Amendment," he said.

"Not if you're lying." I was moving closer

to him now, and my temper was starting to assert itself.

"What did I say in that editorial that wasn't true?" There was an edge in his voice as well now. It was clear that he was no longer amused by my reaction. Good, that made two of us. "Suzanne, you sell death, and you know it. Heart disease is a mass murderer in this country, and you're part of the reason it's so prevalent."

"Seriously? You're actually blaming me for heart attacks?"

"Don't play innocent with me. You contribute to the problem," he said, jabbing his cigarette at me as if it were some kind of knife. "I wasn't lying. I saw what your customer base looked like today."

"Donuts don't kill people," I yelled. "I'm the first to admit that no one should eat them every day, but there's nothing wrong with a treat now and then. Skinny people come to my shop, too, and I know a lot of them did throughout the day today. Did you see them and choose to ignore them, or were you even there?"

"The heavyset outweighed everyone else," he said, pointing at me with his cigarette again.

"What about your cigarettes? Don't you think they're killers?"

"We're talking about donuts, remember? You might as well give up. I'm not about to back down from what I said tonight."

I got up in his face this time. "This isn't over."

I heard Cara from a few feet away. How long had she been standing there? She looked as though she wanted to die as she spoke. "Lester, you've got a call from Mr. MacDonald."

That got his attention. "What does he want?"

"He didn't say. Do you want me to tell him that you're on your break?"

Lester threw the cigarette down and ground it out with his heel. "Don't worry about it. I'll take the call."

"It's line three," she said.

As Lester disappeared back into the building, Cara's tense face blossomed into a smile. "Wow, I thought you were going to slap him there for a second."

"You saw that?" Suddenly I wasn't so proud of my outburst. What had I accomplished, after all? Did I think Lester would air an apology and a retraction if I could bully him into it? Maybe I should have let Momma come along, after all. She might have been able to keep me in check. The fact that I was even considering such an option was enough to tell me that I'd overstepped my bounds. When my mother was the voice of reason, it was time for me to reevaluate my position.

Then again, she could have just as easily led the charge, and things could have turned out even worse.

"I just saw the last bit," Cara admitted.

"Thanks for making up that call, then."

She shook her head. "I didn't. Mr. Mac-Donald owns this station, together with a dozen other investors."

I grinned at her. "Maybe he's a donut fan, and he'll fire Lester."

As Cara hurried back into the building, I realized that I'd done enough damage for one night. I looked at my watch and saw that it was nearly nine. I just had a handful of hours until it was time to get up. I wasn't sure I'd be able to get to sleep, not after what had just happened, but I owed it to myself to try.

As I drove back home, I thought about how personal that attack had been. I knew Lester wasn't a fan of mine, but I had no idea he disliked me that much. Had he come up with his little diatribe on his own, or had someone else put him up to it? I had my share of enemies in April Springs, but small towns could be like that. Sometimes folks took a dislike to someone for no apparent reason, and no doubt a few felt that way about me. But which one of them might have enough influence over Lester to get him to come after me so openly?

I needed to find out, and sooner, rather than later.

My alarm woke me way too early. It had taken some time for me to get to sleep after recapping my confrontation with Lester to Momma. Maybe I'd be able to grab a nap at some point after work. I wasn't sure how many customers I'd have today, given Lester's diatribe on the air. Then again, how many of my customers actually listened to our local radio station, especially at night? Only time would show how effective Lester had been in trying to lead a boycott of Donut Hearts.

I didn't make it to the shop until five after two, late by my normal standards. As I walked past the coffee machine, I hit the start button and then turned on the fryer. It took a while for all that oil to heat up for the first run of donuts at three hundred degrees, and I'd learned early on to start it warming as soon as I walked in the front door.

Emma Blake, my assistant and friend,

wasn't due in for nearly half an hour. That was one bonus I gave her that didn't cost me a dime. She claimed that the extra half hour of sleep was better than any raise I could afford. I checked the answering machine, hoping for a big order in case Lester's call for a boycott worked, but there weren't any messages. Normally I fussed about people who waited until the last minute to order massive amounts of donuts, but I would have gladly taken a spontaneous order at the moment.

I'd have to hurry a little to make up for lost time, but I'd still have plenty of opportunity to mix the batter for the cake donuts, then move on to the yeast donuts, proof them, and be ready when we opened. I always started with the donuts that required a lower oil temperature, and then turned up the heat so I could finish with the yeast donuts.

For the cake donuts, I liked to offer something new every now and then without knocking any of the old favorites off the menu. For example, I offered a peanut donut, a basic cake recipe covered in glaze and then buried in peanuts, but I wanted to try something different that might complement it. The new recipe I was working on was for a peanut butter and jelly donut, something that might be a hit with my younger crowd. I planned on using a peanut-butter-based dough, and was going to try reduced grape jelly as a topping, but so far, I hadn't been able to come up with anything I would be proud enough to sell.

I had just finished mixing the cake donut offerings for the day when Emma walked in, rubbing her eyes as she grabbed her apron. She was young and petite, with a figure I envied but knew I would never emulate, and she had red hair, freckles, and pale blue eyes. "Morning," she said.

"There's coffee," I answered as I added plain cake donut batter to the spring-loaded dropper.

Emma nodded. "Coffee. Yes. Good."

She went out front to get a cup, and I swung the dropper in the air like a pendulum, driving the dough to the extruding point. The donut rounds were dropped straight into the oil, and I always marveled at how perfectly they were formed as they began to fry. It had taken me a while to calculate the right distance to drop them. Too close to the oil and the donuts barely had holes, but alternatively, if I dropped them from too high, they were anything but round by the time they hit the oil.

I'd finished the plain cake and was moving on to the strawberry cake when I realized Emma hadn't even poked her head through the door since she'd gone to get some coffee.

Putting the cleaned dropper aside, I peeked out front to see what was keeping her.

I was surprised to find her sitting at the counter, fast asleep, the mug in front of her forgotten.

My laughter woke her up.

As she lifted her head and rubbed her eyes, Emma asked, "What happened?"

"You dozed off," I said. "If you want to take the day off, I can handle things here on my own today."

Emma stood and stretched. "No, don't worry about me. I'm fine."

"I mean it. It's okay."

"Suzanne, if I'm going to take the day off, I don't plan on getting up at two in the morning to do it. I'm here, and I'm awake. Let's get started."

"You've got a few minutes," I said. "I have a few more cake donuts to make."

"I'll get busy here then."

I finished up the cake donuts for the day, adding half a dozen rounds of my latest peanut butter batter to the fryer. As they fried, I rinsed the dropper, and then called out to Emma. "You can ice them now."

She came in, grabbed the pan, and began icing the cake donuts I'd made, drowning them in a cascade of sugar from the reservoir. I flipped the peanut butter donuts with long chopsticks, and after they were done on both sides, I pulled them out.

Emma noticed the small batch. "Another experiment?"

"You know me. I'm not satisfied unless it's the best." As I put them on the rack to cool, Emma started icing them, as well.

"Just do three," I said. "Leave the other three."

"You're the boss." She took a deep breath. "Should we split one?"

"I haven't made the grape jelly glaze yet," I said.

Emma crinkled her nose at that. "Why ruin them? Why don't we offer them like this and see what happens?"

I grabbed one of the glazed donuts, broke a piece off it, and tasted it.

She was right. It didn't need jelly at all.

It wouldn't be the PB&J I'd planned to offer, but it was certainly a different flavor from the peanut-crusted donuts I'd been selling. I just hoped none of my customers had peanut allergies.

I decided to put one aside for George

Morris, my friend and a good customer who had retired from the police force several years ago. A balding man in his sixties, George had been invaluable during some of my amateur investigations in the past. "Go ahead and glaze the rest of them, but hold one plain donut back for George."

"Just one?"

"He's been complaining about his waistline, so I'm trying not to tempt him too much with free samples."

"I think he looks fine," Emma said.

"Tell him that when he comes in. I'm sure he'd love to hear it. If he comes in, that is."

"Why wouldn't he?" Emma asked as she pulled that last rack of cake donuts off the icing station.

"After Lester Moorefield's rant last night, I'll be surprised if anyone comes through our front door today."

Emma looked confused. "What happened? What did Lester say?"

I brought her up to speed, including my confrontation with him in the radio station parking lot. After I finished, Emma reached for the radio we kept in back.

"What are you doing?" I asked.

"I want to see if they might be rebroadcasting it."

I glanced at the clock, but didn't try to

stop her. WAPS was still off the air, and would be until six A.M., when Lester started his broadcast day.

"Nothing but static," Emma said.

"Trust me, you aren't missing much. I just hope his boycott doesn't work."

She patted my arm. "Don't give it a second thought, Suzanne. Our customers love us too much to turn their backs on us, especially on Lester Moorefield's say-so."

"I hope you're right." His attack had shaken me more than I cared to admit, and self-doubt had begun to creep in. We didn't make a fortune at Donut Hearts on our best days, and there was a fine line between paying our bills plus a little extra and coming under what we needed to meet our daily operating expenses. I'd played with several ideas about how I might increase our income, but nothing had appealed to me. One of my friends and fellow donut makers in Hickory had added a bistro to serve lunch and dinner when the shop wasn't busy making donuts, but he was a trained chef, while I was just a humble donut maker. If I was going to generate any extra income, it would have to be within the confines of the donut world.

At five-thirty, the donuts were ready, displayed proudly in their cases, and we had two different brews of coffee going, along with a carafe of hot cocoa made from my special recipe.

Now all we needed was a customer or two.

As I unlocked the front door, I was surprised to see a police cruiser drive up to the shop. Our chief of police didn't like being seen at my donut shop because of the old jokes about cops and donuts, but some of his officers liked to come by occasionally. One in particular, Stephen Grant, was even becoming a friend, though it was clear Chief Martin wasn't all that thrilled about one of his officers getting chummy with me.

I was in luck, it was my friend; but as Officer Grant got out of his squad car, I knew he wasn't there for an early-morning donut.

There was trouble, and from the expression on his face I had a feeling that, once again, I was right in the middle of it.

# PEANUT BUTTER DROP DONUTS

As I was writing this book, I suddenly realized that I'd never made a peanut-based dough of my own. What better time to explore how, along with Suzanne, to make these. It took a little trial and error, but I've found a recipe that I believe even Suzanne would be proud to serve at Donut Hearts!

## Ingredients

1 egg, beaten
1/2 cup sugar (white)
1/4 cup brown sugar
1 cup buttermilk (2% or whole milk will also do)
2 tablespoons canola oil
1/2 teaspoon vanilla
1 cup all purpose flour
1 tablespoon baking powder
1/4 teaspoon salt
1/2 cup peanut butter (I like chunky, but smooth works fine, too)

## Directions

Heat canola oil to 360 degrees while you mix the batter. Add the sugar slowly to the beaten egg, incorporating it along the way. Then add the milk, oil, and vanilla, stirring well. Sift the dry ingredients and fold it into the batter. Add the peanut butter last, and you're ready.

Take a teaspoon of batter and rake it into the fryer with another spoon. If the dough doesn't rise soon, gently nudge it with a chopstick, being careful not to splatter oil. After two minutes, check, and then flip, frying for another minute on the other side. These times may vary given too many factors to count, so keep a close eye.

Makes around eighteen small donuts

# CHAPTER 2

"What's wrong?" I asked when Officer Grant walked in the door, his frown deepening as he approached me. A thought suddenly occurred to me. "Nothing's happened to Jake, has it?" My boyfriend was in New Bern at the moment, helping the FBI with a sting on some real, honest-to-goodness bad guys. If anything happened to him, I wasn't sure how I'd be able to deal with it. We hadn't been a solid couple all that long, but I couldn't bear the thought of losing him.

"Jake's fine, as far as I know," Officer Grant said, his frown becoming a look of surprise. "Why do you ask?"

"You don't look all that pleased to be here," I said as the relief washed over me. "If it's not Jake, then what's going on? Something's happened, hasn't it?"

"Suzanne, do you mind coming with me?"

I looked at him for a second. "It's not

really a good time. We're just opening the shop, and I can't leave."

He shook his head. "You don't understand. That wasn't a request. The chief needs to see you, and that means right now." He looked around the empty donut shop. "I think Emma can handle things here for a while, don't you?"

I wasn't about to let myself be summoned by Chief Martin without at least asking for the reason. "I'm not going anywhere until I find out what's going on."

Officer Grant nodded. "The chief figured you wouldn't come without a fight. He authorized me to tell you that it involves you directly, but that's all I'm allowed to say right now." Almost as an afterthought, he added, "Trust me; I wouldn't try to strong-arm you if it wasn't important. You know that, right?"

I nodded. "I just don't like being ordered around."

"Tell me about it."

I grabbed my jacket, and then said, "Let me tell Emma before we go." She was still in back doing a round of dishes, and if I knew her, her iPod was on and going full blast.

After I got her attention, she pulled one earbud out and looked at me.

33

"I've got to step out for a while."

She laughed without looking at me. "Where are you going, out dancing?"

"Emma, this is serious. The chief has requested my presence somewhere, and it doesn't look like I can refuse. Watch the front, would you?"

She pulled her hands out of the soapy water. "Should I call my mother to come help out until you get back?"

Emma's mother had stepped in to lend a hand at times when we'd needed her in the past, but I didn't think I'd be gone long enough to make it worth her while to come in. "No, it shouldn't be that bad."

"I hope not, but if you're gone more than thirty minutes, I'm calling her."

"That sounds fine. I'm hoping I won't have any trouble meeting that deadline."

Emma rinsed her hands, and we walked out to the dining area together.

"I just need you, Suzanne," Officer Grant said.

"Trust me; I've got no desire to go wherever you two are going. I'm going to have my hands full running the front," Emma said.

"See you soon," I said as we left. I'd considered grabbing a donut for Officer Grant on the way out, but quickly decided against it. After all, I didn't want to be accused of currying favor with local law enforcement.

I was glad I'd grabbed my jacket. It was still chilly out, and I figured that it wouldn't begin to really warm up until the sun came out.

As we drove away from the shop, I asked, "Where exactly are we going?"

Officer Grant appeared to think about it, and then said, "I don't suppose it could hurt anything to tell you now. We're going to WAPS."

I couldn't believe the nerve of Lester Moorefield. Why had he brought the police into our argument? "I never touched him! Did he say that I did? He's lying. Ask Cara. She saw the entire argument!"

"He didn't say a word."

"Then why are we going to see him?"

Officer Grant let out a deep breath, and then said, "Somebody killed him late last night, Suzanne, and it looks like they might have used one of your pastries to do it."

I couldn't believe what I was hearing. It was like the return of a nightmare I'd lived through once before. "Was it poisoned?"

"No, as far as we know, there wasn't anything wrong with it."

"Then how did it kill him?"

"Suzanne, it looks like he might have choked on it. There was half a box of pastries in the break room."

I paused a moment to take that in. "Then why does the chief need to see me? I can't help it if someone took too big a bite of one of my treats. I can't be held responsible for everything that happens once something leaves my shop."

Officer Grant frowned, and then said, "If you tell anyone I said this, I'll deny it. At first glance, it looked like an éclair was jammed down his throat. It cut off his airway and he couldn't breathe. I don't know what they've found out since. The second the chief saw that pastry, he sent me to get you."

What a terrible way to die. Suffocation couldn't be an easy way to go, and the idea that one of my pastries had been used in a homicide made me feel sick. Something must have showed on my face.

Officer Grant asked, "Are you all right? Maybe I shouldn't have said anything to you about it until we got there."

"I'll be fine," I said. "Do you mind if I crack the window? I could use a little cool air on my face."

"That's fine."

I opened the window, and let the breeze

in. After a minute, I was feeling more like my old self again. It was just in time. I rolled the window back up as we pulled into the parking lot of the radio station where I'd been the night before. Dawn was still an hour away, but heavy-duty lights lined the perimeter, making it as bright as noon. I saw the car Lester had leaned against the night before. Since the entire parking lot was fenced in, there was no need for crime-scene tape anywhere. One of the officers was taking photographs of tire tracks from a drying mud puddle, and I had to wonder if they'd match my Jeep.

At least the body had been removed. I'd looked for it the second we'd pulled up, hoping not to see Lester with my pastry nearby.

I got that wish, but I wasn't off the hook completely.

Chief Martin met me at the car door. Though he'd gained some weight in the past, it was clear that he was working hard at losing it now. I knew he wasn't eating donuts anymore, though he'd never been that big a customer of mine. I wondered if it had something to do with the trouble he was having finalizing his divorce. Word around town was that he and his wife had been living separately for some time, though nothing official had been announced. That's the way it was with small-town living. The grapevine was usually more accurate than the newspaper, and gave up information quicker, too. Sometimes I wondered why Emma's father even bothered running the *April Springs Sentinel.*

Before I could take more than a step away from the cruiser, the chief held an evidence bag in front of my face.

"Is this yours?"

It was clear he wasn't in the mood for small talk. I looked at the remnants of an éclair, studied the custard in the middle, and the shiny chocolate glaze on it. "If I had to guess, I'd say yes, but I could be wrong."

"Who else could have made it?" He was normally gruff with me, but there wasn't even the pretension of civility.

"Chief, someone could have made it in their own kitchen. It's not exactly rocket science. Did you call me for my expert opinion, or did you hear about the argument I had with Lester last night? You don't honestly think I could have done this, do you?"

"I'm not in the opinion business, Suzanne. I'm just interested in facts."

"There's a ringing endorsement if I ever

heard one. Maybe I need to call Jake."

Chief Martin and my boyfriend had a fairly good professional relationship, except when it came to me. They shared a camaraderie, but his association with me put a strain on it at times. "I thought he was tied up somewhere else."

For one second, I'd forgotten all about his trip to New Bern. "Should I call an attorney, then?"

"Do what you please, but I'm not going to arrest you, at least not at the moment." He waved Officer Grant away, and then lowered his voice. "Trust me, I know better than anyone how much Lester loved poking at folks around town with his show. Do you think you're the first person in April Springs he ever went after with that radio program of his?"

"No, but I've got a suspicion that I'm the last."

He nodded. "You've got a point there, and I can't stop people in town from talking, but I'm not about to let it interfere with my investigation."

"Thanks. I appreciate that." Was the chief of police actually acting like a human being for a change?

"That being said, do you have an alibi for last night between ten and two?"

That was more like the chief of police I expected. "I got home about nine-thirty after my argument with Lester, spent half an hour talking about it with my mom, and then I grabbed four hours of sleep before I came into the shop a little after two A.M."

He nodded, and then asked, "Correct me if I'm wrong, but don't you usually go to work a little earlier than that?"

"I slept in a little," I admitted. "As it is, I'm going to need a nap later." A thought suddenly occurred to me. "Have you been checking up on me?"

He didn't even look chastened as he replied. "I've got officers doing night patrols downtown, and one of my men mentioned that your lights were dark at two, when usually they're blazing back in the kitchen by then."

"And he just happened to bring that up this morning, of all days?"

"No, I asked him, Suzanne. I'm investigating a homicide. It's what I do. I keep asking questions until I get answers. And don't knock our patrols. That's how we found Lester."

I frowned at his response. His reply was reasonable, but I still didn't like the idea of anyone checking up on me. "How are you so sure he didn't just choke on a big bite of pastry without help from anyone else?"

"Grant's been talking too much," Chief Martin said as he looked at his subordinate. "I never told you why I was asking about that éclair."

"Don't blame him. You know how relentless I can be."

"I can testify to that. Anyway, we've ruled out choking, either by accident or on purpose. The éclair wasn't what killed him."

Was it wrong that I felt a sense of relief from the news? "What exactly happened, then?"

"The pastry was just the icing on the cake, Suzanne. Lester was strangled from behind, and the éclair was added after the fact."

The weariness I'd been keeping at bay suddenly overwhelmed me. I hadn't been a fan of Lester Moorefield, but that didn't mean I was happy that he was dead. The presence of one of my pastries at the crime scene just added to the exhaustion I felt. "Are you finished with me yet?"

"For now. Hang around a little, I'll have someone drive you back to your shop."

I couldn't bear the thought of lingering at the crime scene for another second if I didn't have to.

"That's okay. I'll call someone," I said.

He seemed to stop caring about me altogether at that point and headed back inside the radio station.

Who could I call? Jake wouldn't be back for a few days, and I knew from experience that he turned his telephone off when he was dealing with something complicated like coordinating a bust with the feds. I thought briefly about phoning Grace, but it was barely past six, and I doubted she'd be up for at least another hour.

I could have called Max, but I'd have to be a lot more desperate than I was right now to telephone my ex-husband.

That left Momma.

I knew she'd be awake, probably sitting at the kitchen table sipping her coffee and reading the scant pages of the *Sentinel.*

I wasn't in the mood for her questions, though.

Maybe I'd just walk.

If I'd gotten an hour more sleep than I had managed, I would have done just that, but I really didn't have any choice, since we'd lost our one taxi service a long time ago.

As I'd expected, she was awake, and answered on the first ring.

"Momma, I need a ride."

"Suzanne, why aren't you at the donut

shop? Did something happen to your Jeep on the way over there? No, you've been gone hours, so it can't be that."

There was no way I was going to get out of an explanation, but I didn't have to do it in the radio station parking lot. Still, I had to give her something. "Lester Moorefield is dead, and someone left one of my pastries on the scene to implicate me. I don't want to get into it now. Could you come to the radio station?"

"I'll be there in six minutes," she said.

While I was waiting, the chief came back out. "Sorry it's taking so long. Do you want me to drive you back myself?"

"Thanks, but Momma's coming for me."

He stood up straighter at the news, and I saw him pull in his stomach, even though my mother was nowhere in sight. The chief had a crush on my mother that dated back to their days in high school, and it was readily apparent to everyone in town that the flames had only grown brighter since.

When Momma drove up, I wasn't all that surprised when the chief walked me to her car.

"Good morning, Dorothy," he said as he tipped his hat to her.

"Hello, Phillip."

"I was wondering if I might have a word

with you?" he asked.

"At this hour? I need to get Suzanne back to her shop."

He wasn't about to be denied, though. "This won't take a second."

Momma put the car in park. "Very well, if you can make it quick."

She got out, and I started to follow them.

Momma wasn't about to allow that, though. "Wait in the car, Suzanne. I won't be a minute. I promise."

As much as I wanted to hear what the chief had to say, I knew that tone of voice. I walked to the car and sat in silence. Just because I wasn't able to eavesdrop didn't mean I couldn't watch them. The chief said something to her, she frowned, shook her head, and then started to walk back to the car. He said something else with some urgency, and she paused just long enough to look back at him for a moment and make one parting comment.

By the time Momma got to the car, I was dying to hear what had been so important about their conversation.

"What was that all about?" I asked.

"I want to hear about what happened to Lester," Momma said.

I wasn't about to let her get away with that. "I saw the way you two were talking.

You weren't discussing the cycles of the moon. What did he have to say?" Before she could reply, I quickly added, "Momma, you know better than anybody in the world that I've got a stubborn streak bigger than yours. Why don't you make it easy on both of us and tell me what just happened."

She mulled that over for thirty seconds, and while she did, I kept my mouth shut. The only thing I could do to wreck it right now was to say something she could use to rebut my argument.

"Very well," she finally said. "He told me he's moved out of his house and filed for divorce. His wife wants out as well, so she's going to Nevada to make it happen quickly."

"So the grapevine's true yet again," I said. "Was that all?"

"Isn't that enough?" Momma asked.

I replayed what I'd seen of their conversation in my mind. "He said something else, didn't he? You weren't pleased to hear it, either."

"Suzanne, were you spying on me?"

I smiled brightly at her. "You bet I was. What else did he say?"

"If you must know, he asked me out to dinner," Momma said.

She was clearly expecting a reaction from me, but I wasn't going to give her one.

After a moment, Momma asked, "Are you telling me that you don't have any comment about that?"

"Yes, ma'am." I paused a second, and then said, "I do have a question, though."

She took a deep breath, and then before I could ask, she said, "I turned him down. No one should be surprised by that."

"Maybe you shouldn't be so quick to dismiss him," I said.

She looked shocked by my response. "I wasn't aware you'd become such a big fan of our chief of police, Suzanne."

"We don't always see eye to eye, but it wouldn't kill you to go out on a date. If you don't like him, pick someone else. Isn't it time you let Dad go?"

She pulled up in front of Donut Hearts, and I could see that Emma had her hands full inside the shop. I should have jumped out and run in to help her, but this was more important to me.

Was that a tear tracking down her cheek? She wiped it away so quickly, I couldn't be certain that I'd seen it at all. "Sometimes I wish I could, but I don't think I can," she said softly.

I touched her arm lightly. "It's not being disloyal, if that's what you're worried about. You deserve to have a life of your own again;

you know that, don't you?"

She frowned and said, "Don't worry about me. I'm happy enough."

"Really? And just exactly how happy is enough?" I asked gently.

She appeared to think about it for a moment, and then shook her head. "You've got customers. You need to go."

"You're more important to me. They can wait," I said.

"Well, I can't," Momma replied, clearly finished with our conversation. "I have a full schedule today, so I'd better get started."

As I started to get out of the car, I said, "I promised you that I'd tell you about Lester. I can hang around and fill you in, if you'd like."

"I know the basics of what happened, and I'm sure the town gossips will fill in the rest. Have a good morning, Suzanne." It was clear that she wanted to get away from me, and the conversation that we'd just had. There was no use arguing with her.

"I hope you do, too," I said as I closed the door. I waved to her as she drove back home, but if she noticed, she failed to return it. I hadn't meant to push my mother so hard, but I worried about her just as much as she worried about me. I knew that moving back in with her after my divorce from Max hadn't been all that easy on either one of us, but we'd come to a good arrangement since then, and most days we got along pretty well.

But what if things kept progressing with Jake? Could I ever leave her alone again? As things stood, I couldn't imagine abandoning her, for whatever reason. So I suppose, in a way, my urging her to jump back into dating had a hint of self-interest in it, as well.

The bottom line, though, was that I wanted her to be happy.

# CHAPTER 3

"What did I miss?" George Morris asked as I walked back into Donut Hearts. I should have known that, given his background in law enforcement, he'd be aware of what was going on before anyone else in town. He'd told me on more than one occasion that he went to bed at night with his police scanner on, listening to what was going on in April Springs, just in case.

"Give me a second," I said as I grabbed my apron from behind the counter. "We can talk about it after the rush."

"I'll be over there when you're ready for me," he said as he pointed to the far end of the counter.

"Who's next?" I asked the waiting line of people.

Emma looked so happy to see me that I thought she might start crying.

After we got through most of our customers together, Emma said, "If it's okay with you, I think I'll get started on more dishes in back."

"That's fine. And Emma?"

"Yes?"

"Thanks for pitching in."

"Glad to," she said as she hurried back into our kitchen. Yet again, I wondered what I would ever do without her.

As I knew he would, George had stuck around. I grabbed one of the experimental donuts I'd made that morning, marveling that it had just been hours ago, and not days. A great deal had happened since I'd worked on that batter.

"Before we get into any details, try this," I said as I offered it to him.

George studied the donut, broke it in half, and then smelled it.

"It's peanut butter," he said.

"Very good. But how does it taste?"

"I don't like peanut butter," George said with a frown.

"Then don't try it," I replied as I tried to get it back from him.

He was too fast for me, though. "Hang on a second. I didn't say I wouldn't at least taste it."

"If you don't like peanut butter, I don't think you'll be able to give it a fair shake, do you? It's no problem, you've tasted enough donuts for me over the years. You can take a pass every now and then. Let me have it and I'll toss it in the trash."

George started to do just that, but at the last second, he popped a bit into his mouth.

"You didn't have to do that," I said.

"Milk," he growled.

I grabbed a pint carton from the fridge and handed it to him. He opened it and took a healthy swallow. Then, after a moment's consideration, George said, "It's not that bad."

"But not good, either, right?"

"I'm not sure." George took another bite, and chased it with milk, as well. "Like I say, it's not bad at all." He finished the sample, then asked, "Do you have any more?"

"I didn't think you were a fan," I said.

"Hey, a guy's got the right to change his mind, doesn't he?"

I couldn't help myself; I laughed. "You are too funny."

George wiped his hands on a napkin, drained the rest of the milk, and then said, "Enough taste-testing, Suzanne. Tell me about what happened."

"Officer Grant came by this morning to take me to the —"

George cut me off. "From the beginning. Start last night. How did you know about the radio commentary?"

"Did you hear it, too?"

"I usually keep it on in the background, but when Lester mentioned this place, I perked right up."

"That's how I heard about it myself."

"I bet you went ballistic," George said with a slight smile.

"Actually, I thought I was pretty calm the way I handled it," I said.

He laughed at that. "Okay, if you say so."

I knew he didn't believe me, and I couldn't blame him. "Fine, I blew up, but who in April Springs would be surprised by that? Not only did he attack my shop, he came after me and my livelihood."

In a gentle tone, he said, "You had plenty of reason to go after him, but it's amazing the chief hasn't locked you up yet."

"He might have ulterior motives for being nice to me," I said, remembering his chat with my mother in the parking lot.

"What do you mean by that?"

Did I really want to get into that with George? "Forget I said anything. I admit that I was mad at Lester last night, but I didn't kill him. That particular thought never even crossed my mind."

"What kind of punishment did?" George asked, a slow smile spreading across his face.

"I considered how much fun it would be to cover him with honey and stake him out on an anthill," I admitted. "Then again, even that much sweetness probably wouldn't make him palatable." What was I doing, speaking ill of the dead like that? I knew better, and I suddenly felt ashamed of my behavior. "Let's just take it for granted that I'm innocent and go from there."

George looked down at the counter, and used his index finger to trace patterns on the top for a few moments before speaking. "Suzanne, I'm guessing we're going to dig into this, right?"

I hadn't had a chance to even catch my breath yet, but I realized I didn't have any choice but to pursue it. Even if the presence of one of my éclairs at the crime scene was purely a coincidence, folks would be looking long and hard at me for the rest of my life if Lester's killer wasn't brought to justice.

"I don't think we have much choice, do you?"

George shrugged. "The chief isn't going to like it."

"Has he ever? I'll do my best not to make him mad, but I'm not making any promises, okay?"

"Okay by me." George stood, pulled a few

dollars from his wallet, and put them on the counter.

I shoved the money back toward him. "Your breakfast is on the house."

"Why should it be?"

I grinned at him. "You're on the payroll again, and all I can afford is coffee, milk, and donuts. Does that work for you?"

He scooped the bills up and tucked them back into his wallet. "Honestly, it sounds pretty darn good."

"Where are you going?" I asked him.

"It's time to start digging."

"Come back at noon and we can come up with a game plan."

"It's a date."

After he was gone, I thought about who might want Lester dead. Besides me, that is. I didn't even know where to start. That wasn't entirely true. His producer, Cara, might be a good source of information. If anyone knew Lester's secrets, and who might have reason to want him dead, it had to be her. As a matter of fact, it might not be a bad idea to give her a call and set up an appointment. Maybe I could take her to lunch at the Boxcar Grill later.

I was dialing the station's number when I put the telephone down. A new wave of customers was coming in, and I had to delay my investigation into Lester's demise. I had a job to do, and it was selling donuts. The investigation would have to wait.

After selling a few random dozen donuts, I decided to make that call while I had the chance.

I wasn't sure she'd still be at the station, but it was the only number I had for Cara. To my relief, she picked up on the fourth ring.

"Hey, Cara. It's Suzanne Hart. I was wondering if you might be free for lunch. It's my treat."

"I really can't afford to say no to a free lunch. I just found out the station manager is seriously thinking about letting me go."

"I'm so sorry," I said.

"It wasn't like I wasn't expecting it. I'm not sure what I'm going to do now. Maybe I can get the new talent to keep me on."

"The lunch offer isn't exactly free," I admitted, my conscience getting the better of me. "I'd like to grill you about Lester."

"Ugh. Do I have to? I've been talking to the police chief most of the morning."

"Of course not," I said. "I'll buy you lunch anyway. How's the Boxcar sound around twelve-fifteen?"

"That would be great. See you there. And Suzanne? I'll answer your questions. You've got a stake in this, too, don't you?"

"More than I'd like."

I was nearly finished for the day as the clock approached noon when a heavyset man dressed in a full-blown clown outfit came in the door. The bright orange fright wig, the greasepainted face, the red rubber ball nose, and the garish outfit gave me the creeps from the second I saw him walking toward the shop in his floppy red oversized shoes.

"Sorry. We're all out of donuts," I said before he could place an order.

"Come on. The display case has plenty left," he said in a whiny voice. I saw a badge on his costume that declared that his name was Officer Zippy. "You can't discriminate against anyone, not even clowns."

I tapped a sign behind the counter and read it to him. "We reserve the right to refuse service to anyone."

"What have you got against clowns, lady?"

I wasn't about to tell him that one of his brethren had ruined my fourth birthday party by scaring the stuffing out of me. I grabbed a glazed donut, shoved it in a bag, and then pushed it toward him. "Here, take this. You can't eat it in here, though."

He shook his head in clear disgust, but he still took the bag and left. I wasn't sure how my customers would react, but I was gratified to hear them applauding as soon as Zippy was gone.

"Sorry about that," I said.

"Are you kidding me?" a heavyset trucker asked. "If he'd sat down, I was out of here. Those guys give me the jitters."

Another diner said, "I don't even think he had a gig. I'm guessing he dresses that way just for fun."

Emma came out at the sound of the commotion. "Is something going on? What did I miss?"

"Not much. Some clown came in here and tried to buy a donut," I said. There was general laughter around the shop at that.

Emma looked perplexed. "What's so funny about that? We get clowns in here all the time."

I couldn't help smiling. "When I say a clown, I mean a clown: makeup, fright wig, and red nose. I threw him out."

The disappointment was clear on her face. "Why did you do that? I happen to love clowns."

There was a chorus of boos generated from her announcement, and Emma shook her head in confusion as she disappeared back into the kitchen. It was no wonder she preferred to stay in the kitchen where life made more sense to her. I thought she was missing out on all the fun.

By the time we were ready to close, there weren't enough donuts left to matter. I bagged them and gave them to Emma. "Why don't you take these over to your dad?"

"I'm sure he'd love it, but Mom's got him on another diet."

I didn't need the calories, either. It was too tempting to taste the fresh donuts as they got their shower of glaze; taking home leftovers was out of the question. They would sit there in the bag calling me until I'd eaten every last one of them.

"That's fine. I'll just give them to George."

"Give George what?" a familiar voice said as he came into the shop.

"Speak of the devil, and he appears," I said with a smile.

"Not sure I like the comparison," George said as he sat at the bar.

"Let me make it up to you." I slid the bag of donuts toward him.

He peeked inside, and then smiled. "On second thought, call me whatever you like. Suzanne, do you have a second?"

"Just that. Can we talk while I work? I need to clean up. I'm meeting Cara for lunch to see if I can get any information out of her about Lester."

"I was going to suggest that myself. Nice thinking." I saw his glance dart back to the bag.

I grinned at him and served him a cup of coffee. "Go ahead and have one."

"Maybe a bite," he said as he pinched off a piece of éclair. I wasn't sure I'd ever be able to eat one of those particular pastries ever again, but if it bothered George, he didn't show it.

I locked the door and flipped the sign to the world that there would be no more donuts, at least for today. "Emma, if you'll sweep up out here and clean the tables, I'll handle the rest of the dishes."

"That's a deal," she said. "There's not much left back there, anyway."

"Thanks. I'll see you tomorrow."

"Bright and early," she said.

George and I disappeared into the kitchen, and I decided I could knock the dishes out and still make my lunch with Cara.

"If you want to go ahead while I work, I'd love to hear what you've found out," I said.

As I started the water in the sink, George said, "I hate to admit it, but I haven't had too much luck so far."

"That's fine. You haven't had much time."

George looked frustrated. "That's not it.

59

It appears our chief of police had a feeling I'd be helping you investigate this. He's blocked my access to the police department, Suzanne. All I could find out before he shut me out was that Lester had more enemies than they can count, but we already knew that, didn't we? I would have found out more, but Martin kicked me out of headquarters before I could do much more digging."

He was clearly hurt by the move, and I wondered what price he was paying for having helped me in the past. "I'm so sorry."

He shrugged, finished his coffee, and said, "It's not your fault."

"We both know better than that. Why don't you sit this one out? I can do a little digging myself, and I'm sure Grace will be more than willing to help."

George shook his head. "There's not much I can do about the police chief, but I've got some contacts of my own. It's just going to be a little tougher this time, that's all."

I was about to insist that he drop it, but one look at his eyes told me that would be the wrong thing to say. Since George had retired from the force, I knew he missed many aspects of his old job. There was power in knowing what was going on behind the scenes, and he'd always been more than generous using his connections to gather information for me in the past. "Don't let him get you down, then," I said, "but even if you can't access your usual sources, I can still use your insight and deductive skills."

He raised an eyebrow as he studied me. "Suzanne, you're not patronizing me, are you?"

"Are you kidding? I'm as sincere as I can be. Regardless of whether you can run criminal records or snoop through files, you've got instincts I depend on."

"I'll see what I can do to make my contributions more than that." He glanced at the clock. "What time's that lunch of yours with Cara?"

I looked up. "I'm going to be late if I don't leave right now." I'd heard Emma leave a few minutes before, and I began to regret letting her go. I hated having dirty dishes sit on the counter or even in the sink, but there was nothing I could do about it. I threw my dishrag down on the counter, and George swooped it up.

"Go on, you don't want to be late. Don't worry about the dishes. I'll finish them for you," he said.

"I couldn't ask you to do that."

"Come on, Suzanne, it will give me some

time to think about my next move, and if I'm able to give you a hand, so much the better."

I kissed him on the cheek. "I'd try to talk you out of it, but my heart just wouldn't be in it." I handed him a spare key. "Lock up when you leave, okay?"

"Good luck."

"Thanks."

I started to grab my jacket, but knew that temperatures had warmed up substantially since I'd taken that predawn ride in the police cruiser. It was a lovely day as I made my way up the tracks to the Boxcar Grill. The walk there was an easy and natural path, since my converted train depot and the diner were both poised near the long-forgotten railroad tracks, its steel rails now buried in the grass. I often wondered about who had traveled the line when it had been active. Rail travel had long fascinated me, and I kept threatening to close the donut shop for a couple of weeks and fly to Canada for a vacation I could only dream about. There was a train ride up there through the Canadian Rockies that looked amazing, but I knew it was just a pipe dream. I couldn't even keep the shop closed one day a week like any sane and rational person would do, instead choosing to go it alone and give my assistant the day off. Two weeks off from work was simply out of the question. I'd wanted to take that trip as a honeymoon when I'd married Max, but he'd been more interested in going to Hollywood. Like an idiot, I'd gone along with the plan, only to discover that he'd scheduled two auditions while we were there. The Great Impersonator had struck again, and I wondered how I didn't realize that our marriage was doomed from the start. I was probably still seeing the world through love-tinted glasses; looking back on it now, I found it hard to believe that I'd ever really been that naïve.

"Someone's here waiting for you," Trish Granger said as I walked into the Boxcar Grill. Trish and I had been friends almost as long as Grace and I had. She was fit and trim, and her blond ponytail was neatly in place, as always. She'd worn her hair down a handful of times over the years, and each time I marveled about how different — and how foreign — she looked.

"What can I say? I'm a popular woman," I said as I looked around the long counter and the line of booths. Most of the booths and several of the seats at the counter were taken. It took me a second to spot Cara.

"Do you need a menu?" Trish asked me

as I started toward the booth Cara had captured.

"Have I ever needed one?" I asked Trish with a grin.

"I make other things besides cheeseburgers, you know," she said.

"Not as far as I'm concerned."

I said hello a few times as I made my way through the intimate space. I thought I'd known a lot of people growing up in April Springs, but it amazed me how many people I came into contact with running Donut Hearts. Grace had been trying to convince me to run for mayor, but I had enough on my hands just running the shop and trying to stay out of trouble without adding the town's troubles to my plate.

As I joined her, I said, "Thanks for meeting me, Cara."

She smiled. "Are you kidding? This is a real treat for me. I don't get out much."

"You must not," I said with a smile of my own, "if I'm considered a treat."

"Don't sell yourself short, Suzanne." Cara picked up a menu and studied it for a moment before realizing that I didn't have one. "Do you want to share?"

"No, thanks. I'll have a meal by myself."

"I meant the menu."

"I know you did," I said. "It's just my odd

sense of humor. I don't need to see a menu. I get the same thing every time I come."

Cara nodded and put her menu on the table. "Then I'll have what you're having."

"Wow, that's a bold move. What if I order a squid sandwich?"

"I didn't see one on the menu, but I'm in a real risk-taking mood. Besides, you're the one buying."

I laughed, happy to be sharing her company. I knew she hadn't been fond of Lester, but I still wasn't sure how she'd react to our lunch. She seemed in good spirits. Death did that to people sometimes. It made them realize how precious life really was.

Trish approached with an order pad. "Are you ready?"

"My regular, times two."

She nodded, then looked at Cara. "You're just encouraging her, you know that, don't you?"

After Trish went to place our order, I could see a slip of concern show on Cara's face. I didn't want her on edge just before I was going to grill her. "Don't worry. I usually get a cheeseburger, fries, and a Coke."

She looked relieved. "That sounds great." Cara adjusted her place mat until it was perfectly aligned with the tabletop. "Now, what would you like to know about Lester?"

"It can wait until after we eat," I said.

She shook her head. "If it's all the same to you, I'd just as soon get it over with so we can enjoy our food."

"Fair enough. What can you tell me about the man that I might not already know?"

"Besides his penchant for shooting off his mouth?" She must have realized how callous that sounded. "Sorry. I'm so used to complaining about him that I keep forgetting it's not polite to speak of the dead that way."

Trish brought us our drinks, and after she was gone, I lowered my voice. "If you could suppress that feeling for a few minutes, I'd appreciate it."

She nodded. "Okay, I get it. Let's see, what is there to say about my former boss? He had a temper, but I don't have to tell you that, and he enjoyed nothing more in the world than going after people with his editorials."

"Anybody in particular? I wasn't a big fan, and he usually ran his spots after my bedtime."

"Are you kidding? You were just his latest target. In the past four days, he's gone after the mayor, one of our town councilwomen, and a shady businessman from Hudson

Creek. What he did to you was gentle compared to the way he went after them."

"Do you think one of them could have had something to do with Lester's death?" I still had a hard time calling it murder.

She played with her straw for a second, and then said, "I honestly couldn't say."

"So, there's no shortage of people for my list."

"It might be easier coming up with folks who didn't want to see him pay for his actions and attitude."

I took a sip of my drink, and then asked, "Can you think of anything else he might have been into that could have gotten him into trouble?"

She appeared to think about that for a few seconds before answering. "The only other person I can think of who might have wanted to see him dead is his wife."

"What?" I nearly spilled my Coke. "Lester was married?"

Cara nodded. "It surprised me, too, when I found out. They haven't lived together in ten years, but for some reason, they never got a divorce. She called the station once. I thought Lester was going to have a heart attack."

"Do you know anything about her?"

Cara frowned. "Not really. Her name is

Nancy Patton, and she lives in Union Square. I've never met the woman, but she surely was able to push his buttons. If I were digging into this myself, I'd talk to her."

"What makes you think I'm investigating what happened to Lester?" Were my actions that transparent to the rest of the world?

She shook her head. "You don't have to pretend with me. Why else would you care about Lester? Not that I blame you. He was just my boss, but if I'd had a reason to want him dead, I'd probably be looking into who killed him myself."

That was an interesting point. "You had to work with him every day. That has to make you a suspect in the eyes of the police, too."

She frowned. "I don't think so, but I could be wrong. The chief questioned me, but Lester was my paycheck, for all intents and purposes. I'm going to have a hard time finding a job making anywhere near what I was pulling in from the station. The last thing I ever wanted was for something bad to happen to Lester. Besides, I wasn't even at the station when it must have happened. I was at home with my kids. I only get them once a month, and I'm not about to waste a visit."

"You should be okay, then."

Our food came, and we switched topics to make the meal more pleasant. After a nice lunch during which we avoided talking about Lester completely, I picked up the check, and Cara thanked me as she left.

I had paid the bill and was saying good-bye to Trish when the last person in the world I wanted to see suddenly blocked my way out the door.

# OATMEAL/RAISIN/CRANBERRY DONUTS

This recipe is one where I got carried away. I started with a basic recipe, and then added oatmeal. That was good, and since I love oatmeal raisin cookies, I added a handful of raisins, as well. I was scrounging in my pantry one day and found dried cranberries, so I decided to add them to the mix. A lot of folks might add nuts to this recipe, but I'm not a fan, so I skip them. These are really tasty, and are pretty, too!

## Ingredients

1 egg, beaten
1/2 cup sugar (granulated white)
1/2 cup milk (2% or whole milk will do)
2 tablespoons canola oil
1/2 teaspoon vanilla
1/4 teaspoon cinnamon
1 cup all purpose flour
1 teaspoon baking powder
1/2 teaspoon baking soda
1/4 teaspoon salt
2 tablespoons oatmeal (old-fashioned, not quick)
2 tablespoons raisins
2 tablespoons dried cranberries

## Directions

Heat canola oil for frying to 360 degrees while you mix the batter. Add the sugar slowly to the beaten egg, incorporating it along the way. Then add the milk, oil, and vanilla, stirring well. Sift the dry ingredients, but hold out the oatmeal, raisins, and cranberries for last. Add the dry ingredients to the wet, and then fold in the extras, until the batter is smooth.

When the ingredients are incorporated, take a teaspoon of batter and rake it into the fryer with another spoon. If the dough doesn't rise soon, gently nudge it with a chopstick, being careful not to splatter oil. After two minutes, check, and then flip, frying for another minute on the other side. These times may vary given too many factors to count, so keep a close eye on the donuts.

Makes around eighteen small donuts.

# CHAPTER 4

"What are you doing here, Max?" The last I'd heard, my ex-husband, Max — also known as the Great Impersonator — had left town for California, hoping to increase his presence in national commercials. He'd claimed to be a serious actor from the moment we'd met, but the only things I'd ever seen him acting in were thirty- and sixty-second spots. He was handsome as ever, and I wondered if karma would ever work on him and he'd finally start to show his age. So far, no such luck.

"Come on, aren't you glad to see me?" He gave me the grin that had melted my heart once upon a time, but no more.

"About as happy as I would be getting audited by the IRS," I said. "Do you want to move, or do I have to go through you? Either way is fine with me."

His smile faltered a little. "Can't we at least be friends? I know Bishop is in your life now, but that doesn't mean the two of us can't at least be cordial to each other."

"Fine. We're friends."

He didn't budge. Instead, Max stuck out his hand and grinned at me. "Let's shake on it."

Trish came up beside me. "Everything okay, Suzanne? I've got a brand-new Taser behind the counter, and it's fully charged. I'd love to have a chance to try it out."

Max pulled back his hand and put both up in the air in capitulation. "No need for violence, ladies. I can take a hint; I'm moving. Is it okay if I grab a table now?"

"As long as you behave yourself," Trish said, softening her scowl to a smile.

"That I can't promise," Max replied, his grin back at full wattage.

After he was gone, I said to Trish, "Sorry about that. He always seems to bring out the worst in me."

"What else are exes good for?" Trish asked. "You don't have to apologize to me, especially not when it comes to Max."

I left the Boxcar, and wondered how Jake was getting along as I walked back toward my shop. I missed him, but I realized how important his job was to him. It kept him on the road too many days, but my boyfriend was literally keeping the bad guys off the streets, so I couldn't exactly complain about it. Compared to what I did, he was a world saver. Not that donuts didn't add a little joy to people's days. I wasn't one to underestimate the power of a good pastry, but I wasn't kidding anybody. Nobody's life was going to change because of one of my treats.

I was nearly back at the donut shop to see if George had finished washing those dishes when I saw a car I knew parked in front.

Grace was sitting inside, and I couldn't have been happier to see her. Besides being my best friend, she'd been my partner in crime in the past, investigating cases off the police chief's radar, and I needed her now, more than ever.

The second Grace saw me, she popped out of her car and hugged me. "You are a trouble magnet, young lady," she said as she pulled away.

"It does seem to find me. Sorry I didn't call this morning as soon as I found out about Lester."

"You're forgiven," she said. "You wouldn't have reached me, anyway. I was out of town."

"Business?" I asked.

"It surely wasn't pleasure. I've got an employee in Asheville I'm going to have to fire if she doesn't shape up, and fast. Who knew being a supervisor was going to be such a pain? It's seriously cutting into my own slack time."

"You could have gone to San Francisco," I reminded her.

"All in all, I'd rather be here, even with the headaches. So, word around town is that you shoved a pastry down Lester Moorefield's throat. Do you need an alibi? Or how about ten thousand dollars in unmarked bills and a passport in someone else's name?"

"Do you have either one of those on you?" I asked her with a smile.

Grace pulled out her wallet. After a second, she said, "How about seventy-three dollars and one of my old expired driver's licenses?"

"I'll pass. I could use your help, though, unless you're too busy with work."

"Hey, I'm the boss now, remember? I'll work it out. What can I do to help?"

"I just found out Lester Moorefield is still married to a woman in Union Square, and I need to pay her a visit. Care to come along?"

"What are we waiting for?" Grace asked. That was just one of the things I loved about my best friend. If I needed her, she was there. There were no questions, no qualifiers, just a ready yes every time I asked.

"I just want to check one thing first," I said. "Do you mind coming into the shop for a second?"

"Why don't I make a few phone calls out here while you're inside," she suggested. "I've got to clear a few things off my calendar."

I suddenly felt guilty about taking up so much of her time. "I don't want to put you out, Grace."

"Nonsense. I've been looking for an excuse to do something rash, and this sounds perfect."

I went inside Donut Hearts and headed straight for the kitchen. The dishes were drying on a towel, and there was a note from George.

*"Sorry I missed you. Hope your lunch was productive. I'm going to try something different. I'll check in later. George."*

It felt good knowing my friends were rallying around me. If news of Lester's demise had spread through town yet, it hadn't affected my sales for the day. I wasn't surprised that we hadn't sold many éclairs, though.

At least my customers were sticking with me.

For now.

As we drove toward Union Square in my Jeep, Grace asked, "What exactly happened last night?"

"How did you hear about that?"

She grinned at me. "Come on, Suzanne. You should know how small a town April Springs is better than most folks around here. Do you honestly think no one saw you screaming at Lester outside the radio station?"

I hadn't realized that my confrontation with him had been so public. "I know Cara heard part of our argument, but I didn't realize anyone else was listening. Has she been talking about what happened?"

"No, I heard it from Kate Baylor. She was walking her dogs and happened past just as you were reaming Lester out. She told me she wanted to applaud, but she didn't want to startle Monet and Degas. Those dogs are jumpy."

It figured that someone had witnessed my diatribe. "I can't get away with anything in this town, can I?"

"It should be enough to keep you on your toes, but it doesn't seem to work that way.

What's our cover story going to be this time? Can we be spies? I'd love to be mysterious. I can totally pull that off, don't you think?"

I laughed. "If anyone can, it's you. I thought we'd use a simple approach; sorry about your loss and all that. After we offer our condolences, we can ask her questions about her late husband."

Grace apparently didn't like that approach. Although she was always there for me, she didn't necessarily go along with every idea I had. After all, what fun would that be? "Why should she talk to us? We have to have a good reason to interrogate her."

I thought about that, and realized Grace had a point. Sometimes subterfuge was a handy way of getting someone to trust us.

"We could always be reporters again," I said.

"No, we've done that. I don't want to work for a newspaper again."

I laughed. "You know we're not actually writing a story, don't you?"

"It should be a little more glamorous than that; that's all I'm saying."

Inspiration suddenly struck. "How about if we claim we represent *Radio World* magazine? We can say we're doing a tribute to

Lester for the next issue and we need background from her."

Grace thought about that for a handful of seconds. "Is there really such a magazine?"

"With the Internet these days, who's to say? It can be an online start-up thing, and no one will ever know the difference."

"Fine. You can be the reporter, though."

"What will you be?" I asked.

She reached into her bag and pulled out a small digital camera. "I'm the photographer assigned to the story."

"With that?" I asked. "It's not much of a camera."

"It's digital," she answered. "You'd be amazed by how powerful it is."

"I don't doubt it. I'm just saying that it's not all that impressive to look at."

"Trust me, she won't know the difference."

It just might work at that. Neither of us was all that savvy about what real writers and photographers looked like, and we had to assume that none of the people we were going to be "interviewing" knew, either.

As I drove into Union Square, Grace asked, "How exactly are we going to find this woman? Do you know where she works?"

"I've got a source we can use," I said as I

parked in front of Napoli's Restaurant. It had long been my favorite place, and Jake and I had had our first date at the Italian restaurant.

"Are you going to check the telephone book?"

"I can do better than that. If anyone knows about someone in Union Square, it's got to be the DeAngelis clan. I have great faith in Angelica and her daughters."

Grace nodded as we got out, but as soon as we approached the door, she said, "Too bad they aren't open yet."

"I'm not giving up that easily." I pounded on the door, and a minute later, Maria, one of the daughters, came out. "Sorry, we're closed . . . oh, Suzanne, how are you?" Maria was an olive-skinned beauty like her sisters and mother, and I always enjoyed seeing her.

After she hugged me, I said, "I'm good. How's your mother?"

"She's on the warpath at the moment, but at least I'm not the one in her sights," Maria said with a smile. "Hi, Grace," she said as she glanced over at my friend.

"Hey, Maria. Sorry to just barge in like this."

She smiled. "Friends and diversions are always welcome. How can we help?" We'd stepped inside the restaurant, shutting out the strip mall outside and entering a world with a sparkling fountain, deep red carpet, and faded brass fixtures. The windows were covered with heavy draperies, and the bright April sun was completely blocked out.

"We're looking for information about someone here in Union Square," I said.

Maria nodded. "You should ask Momma. She knows everyone around here. Back this way; she's in the kitchen," she said as she led us past the tables and through the swinging doors.

The change in atmosphere was striking, and instant. There was real brightness in the kitchen, with stainless steel everywhere and strong overhead lights illuminating the place as if it were an operating room. Angelica was chastising one of her daughters as we walked in, the two of them leaning over a marble slab while working dough, as Antonia looked on. Angelica was lecturing her youngest. "Sophia, you have to be gentle with the dough. It responds to the emotion you have while you're creating it."

"It's just pasta," Sophia said, and I saw Maria and Antonia both wince.

Angelica suddenly dropped the ball of dough she'd been working with her hands on the slab. "Just pasta? It is what makes us special. Without this, we are just another restaurant. We are —" Angelica noticed us then, and her tirade was cut short. "Ladies. How lovely. Let me make you something to eat."

"Hi, Angelica. We're not here for lunch. We're looking for some information."

"Speak for yourself," Grace said. "I'm starving."

"Grace," I said firmly, but Angelica only laughed.

"We can eat and talk at the same time, no? What sounds good?"

"Anything you make," I said as my stomach rumbled. No matter how full I might be, being around Angelica always made me hungry.

Angelica looked around, and her gaze settled back on the dough. "I normally let it cure, but let's have fresh pasta."

"Wonderful," I said as I took a seat by the counter. Grace was quick to join me.

"Do you mind if I work while we talk?" Angelica asked. It was clear to see where her daughters got their good looks, even if Angelica had sampled too much of her own divine cooking over the years to fit into any of their dresses.

After she measured out flour and a pinch of salt, Angelica made a reservoir, cracked a couple of eggs, and added them to the mix. As she stirred the eggs into the flour, she turned to me. "Go ahead and ask. I can talk while I work."

"We're looking for Nancy Patton," I said.

A cloud crossed her normally sunny face.

"I'm sorry," I said. "Did I say something wrong?"

"That woman is poison," Angelica said with passion as she mixed the eggs more and more thoroughly into the flour. When she was satisfied with the blending, she added a teaspoon of cold water, stirred again, added a touch more water, and when it was mixed in, as well, she nodded as she turned to her daughter. "That's perfect just the way it is. Do you see that, Sophia?"

"Yes, Momma," all three daughters present said in unison, as if by rote.

Angelica studied them, each in turn, to see if they were having fun at her expense, but quickly saw that they spoke more from habit than anything else.

"What makes her poison?" I asked.

"She thinks the world owes her something, and she's honor-bound to collect her payment in full. She runs a consignment shop in town and carries all kinds of things for sale. There are people around here who believe she charges much more than she should, and takes more than the percentages she promises."

"Have you ever sold anything with her?" I asked, fascinated by this woman's practiced hands at work. Angelica shook her head as she slapped the ball of dough down and then began shaping it with a tapered maple rolling pin. It was much like the one I'd had, and ruined, saving myself from a murderer. I'd bought half a dozen replacements, but none of them were as good as the one that had been destroyed. Maybe, given enough time, one would form to my palms like the other had, but I doubted it.

Once Angelica was satisfied with the thickness and consistency, she took out an automatic roller and set it to its widest opening. As she turned the crank and fed the dough through, it became more and more consistent in its texture. She ran the dough through, folded it once, and then gave it a half turn and did it again.

"We stay away from her," Angelica said. She turned to her daughters and asked, "Have any of you had any experiences with her?"

"Besides the time she came in here and insisted on a free meal because we were three minutes later than she thought we should be?" Antonia asked.

"That doesn't count," Angelica said.

"How about when she tried to sell Bonnie Prescott's freezer as new and keep the profit for herself?" Sophia asked.

"Do you know that happened for a fact?"

"No," her daughter reluctantly admitted.

"Then it's nothing you can prove." Angelica changed the setting on the machine, and the dough became thinner and thinner with each pass. When she was satisfied, she changed heads on the rolling machine and began cutting long strands of pasta out of the sheets. Wrapping them up loosely on her rolling pin, she went to a pot of boiling water and slid it all gently in. "Did you see that, Sophia?" she asked her daughter, who'd been watching carefully. "How delicately I introduced the pasta to the water?"

"Yes, Momma," she said, and I saw the other daughters mouthing the words as well, though this time they kept their chorus of responses to themselves.

"We have three minutes," Angelica said. Maria, Antonia, and Sophia swung into action, setting the counter with real butter and parmesan cheese, along with six plates and wine glasses.

Angelica removed the pasta, drained it, added a touch of olive oil, some butter, and oregano, and then tossed it all together.

There was plenty for all of us, and as we were served, Maria provided a touch of wine, as well.

It was one of the best meals I'd ever had in my life.

When we were finished, Angelica smiled lovingly at her daughter. "And that's the way it's done."

Sophia nodded, the understanding reflected in her gaze at her mother.

"Can we pay you for this delicious meal?" I asked as I stood.

Angelica looked hurt. "You would pay for friendship? No, not in my restaurant."

"Well, I can't get you to come over and eat donuts at my place," I said. "It's not exactly fair, is it?"

Angelica seemed to think about that, and then said, "You make a point. We will gladly accept your offer someday."

"Soon," I said.

"Soon."

As Grace and I stood at the door, I asked, "Where exactly is this woman's consignment shop?"

"You can't miss it," Angelica said. "It's between Auntie's Antiques and the barbershop. It's called Second Acts. What a name."

"Thanks again."

"Come back anytime, and bring that fellow of yours with you. I love to watch him eat. You're lucky with that one."

"I know, but let's not tell him, okay?"

Angelica smiled at me. "I have a feeling he knows how lucky he is, too. Don't wait so long to come back next time, Suzanne. You, too, Grace."

"We promise," I replied.

After we were back in the Jeep, Grace said, "I don't think I've ever had anything so good in my life."

"She makes magic with some flour, a few eggs, and a pinch of salt, doesn't she?"

"You're no slacker, either," Grace said.

"I wasn't fishing for compliments."

"Good, then I won't have to give you one. It is hard to believe, though, that you two use so many of the same ingredients. Are you ready to tackle Nancy Patton?"

I wasn't entirely sure at the moment. "It's almost not worth spoiling that great lunch, you know what I mean? Seriously, if she was married to Lester and they couldn't stay together, how bad must she be?"

"I'm afraid there's only one way we're going to find out."

We drove a few blocks to the heart of downtown, and Second Acts was right where we'd been told.

I took a deep breath, and then turned to

Grace as I parked.

"Remember, I'm the reporter, and you're the photographer."

"Got it," she said, taking her camera out as we walked to the front door.

A woman younger than I'd been expecting was behind the desk of the store. She was more handsome than pretty, with razor lips and a blunt nose that still managed to convey that she was more put together than anyone else on the planet. I had a hard time imagining her with Lester, but then again, who knew what brought people together.

As I glanced around the room at the hodgepodge of items she had for sale, I wondered how she managed to stay in business. At first glance, it looked as though a yard sale had exploded inside, but as I looked a little closer, I saw some really nice things mixed in with the clutter. Something in particular caught my eye. It was a genuine Houpt donut cutter, a different model from the one I owned. An aluminum cylinder the size of a can of peas offered a grid of raised edges for cutting donuts out of dough simply by rolling it across the surface with its wooden handle. It surprised me to see that it was nicer than the one I was currently using. Although Grace and I had a cover story all worked out, in an instant, I decided to abandon it. I had a new plan, and if the price was anywhere near reasonable, I was going to have a new donut cutter, as well.

I turned and winked at Grace, and then picked up the cutter. It was marked $65, and in all honesty, I wasn't sure if that was a good price or not. I held it up to the woman and asked, "Is there any room to negotiate on this price?"

"Bring it here," she commanded.

I obeyed, and she took the cutter from my hand. After studying a cryptic code on its handle, she said, "The price is firm, but I can allow a ten percent discount."

I was about to say that it really wasn't all that firm after all, when common sense took over. I was trying to ingratiate myself with her by being a paying customer.

"That's most gracious of you. I'll take your kind offer."

She nodded her approval and began the paperwork, no doubt to credit the sale to the proper client.

"You look awfully familiar," I said as she worked. "Have we met?"

She flicked her glance my way. "I doubt it."

It wasn't the warmest response in the world, but I offered my hand anyway. "I'm

Suzanne Hart. I run the donut shop in April Springs."

"I wouldn't know about that. I don't eat them," she said severely.

Wow, I was feeling all warm and fuzzy from her gushing about my livelihood.

It was time to lie. I snapped my fingers and said suddenly, "I've got it. You were with Lester Moorefield when I saw you. You two were close, weren't you?"

She shrugged, not even trying to feign an answer now. Perhaps it had been a mistake abandoning the plan Grace and I had come up with, but it was too late now. Or was it? Maybe I could modify it to make it work.

As I slid the money for the cutter to her across the counter, I said, "I also write freelance articles for a few magazines. As a matter of fact, I've been approached to write something on Lester." It was time to dive in and worry about the consequences later. "You two were married, weren't you?"

Her pen stuttered across the receipt, and I knew I'd gotten her attention, at least for a moment. "Not were. Are."

She was using her words as though they cost her money, at least with me.

I was about to say something when Grace said just behind me, "Oh, no. I can't believe

90

nobody told you. I'm so sorry, but he's dead."

The woman looked at Grace as though she'd just slapped her. "I'm sure you're mistaken."

"I'm afraid she's not," I said. "The police found him this morning."

Nancy Patton started to take a step forward, and then suddenly thought better of it. "I'm not feeling well," she said just before she collapsed into my arms.

# CHAPTER 5

"Great job. You killed her," I told Grace as I tried to keep Nancy, and me, from falling to the floor. She hadn't looked all that heavy before, but as dead weight, she felt like a sack of rocks in my arms.

"She's not dead," Grace said. "She couldn't be. The woman just fainted, Suzanne. There's no reason to overreact."

"Do you mind giving me a hand before we both topple over?" I asked.

Grace offered a quick hand, and we moved Nancy to a nearby sofa. The FOR SALE sign got a little crumpled as we put her down, but that was the least of my worries. Could she have a bad heart? If she did, the shock Grace had just given her might have been enough to push her over the edge. I couldn't wait any longer for her to come to on her own. I started to dial 911 when Grace saw what I was doing. "Hang on a second. Let me try something else first."

There was a glass of water on the desk, and she got it and flicked a good amount of it into Nancy's face. It took a second, but her eyelids finally began to flutter, and she woke up.

"What happened?" she asked as she looked at us both. Her gaze turned suspicious as she asked, "Did you two drug me?"

"You fainted," I said, surprised to hear what her first notion was about us. There wasn't a whole lot of trust there.

Grace leaned in and added, "I'm so sorry that we were the ones who told you."

Nancy's face reddened. "I had to hear it eventually. It was such a shock hearing it blurted out like that."

"I'm sure it was," Grace said.

"Who would want to see him dead, Nancy?" I asked.

She shook her head as though to clear the cobwebs, then took a few moments to compose herself. "Lester always had a way of bringing out the worst in people, you know? It could be anybody he's offended. The police should look into his editorials and question those people he exposed most recently."

I wasn't about to volunteer the information that I'd been the last one in his sights. "I'm sorry for your loss."

She dabbed at a tear as she said, "I just can't believe he's really gone. What happened to him?"

"He was choked," I said, having no desire to divulge that one of my pastries had been jammed into his mouth. It hadn't killed him, even the police knew that, though I had to wonder if most folks in April Springs would believe that it wasn't my éclair that had done him in, no matter what the official cause of death was.

"That sounds dreadful." Her face went even paler at the news, and I was beginning to worry that she might be on her way to passing out again.

It was essential to ask questions while she was still conscious. "Your arrangements were unusual, wouldn't you say?"

She frowned at me as she answered. "I don't see how. There are many married couples who choose to live apart in different areas."

"It's usually more bicoastal than towns half an hour apart, though. I've known Lester for years, and I just found out about you today."

Nancy shrugged. "It worked for us. We never felt the need to explain anything to anyone else."

Lester's widow was starting to get some

of her bristle back, and I knew that I had to speak quickly if I was going to find out anything else. "Besides his radio program, can you think of any other ways he might have antagonized someone?"

Nancy appeared to think about it, and then she said, "Nothing, unless this has something to do with his book."

"What book?"

Nancy's smile lacked warmth as she explained, "The last time we spoke, Lester told me that he was writing an exposé on someone in April Springs that would blow the lid off the town. He was more excited about it than I'd seen him in years." She paused, and then added, "Then again, I never could read the man. There might be no book at all."

This was news to me. "Any idea who it might have been about?"

"Not a clue, and if I know Lester, it won't be easy to figure out. He played things pretty close to the vest, even with me." Another tear tracked down her cheek. "I know it's going to strike a great many people as odd, but I'm going to miss him."

"Since you two are married, I suppose you'll inherit everything," Grace said. She'd been standing there so quietly listening to us that I'd nearly forgotten she was there.

"I'm not concerned about that at the moment." Nancy stood and brushed imaginary wrinkles out of her outfit. "If you'll excuse me, I need to close the shop. I suppose I have to see to the arrangements."

As she hustled us both out, I was nearly to the door when it occurred to me that I was forgetting something. I wasn't about to leave without the cutter I'd just bought, and I walked back to the desk to retrieve it.

Nancy looked annoyed to see that I wouldn't leave. "What is it? I'm afraid I have a great deal of work to do before I lock the doors."

"I almost forgot my donut cutter," I said.

She put a hand on it before I could pull it away. "After you pay for it, it's yours."

"But I already paid you in cash," I said.

She looked at me skeptically. "I'm sorry, but I don't believe so. Did I give you a receipt?"

What was she trying to pull here? "You were writing one when my friend told you about your husband."

Nancy pretended to look through a pile of papers on her desk. "I don't see it. Sorry, I wish I could help."

I could see that Grace was about to explode when I said calmly, "Let's call the police. I'm sure they can straighten this out.

Once you balance your cash drawer, you'll see that you already collected my money for it."

When Nancy realized that we weren't backing down, she looked once more on her desk. What a surprise. She suddenly "found" my nearly completed receipt after all. I took the cutter from her, as well as the receipt, and thanked her for her time.

Once we were outside, Grace said, "She's got nerve trying to steal your money right out from under your nose. From what we've heard, the woman's consistent, if nothing else; I have to give her that."

"I can't believe she could lie so convincingly. If I hadn't seen her take my money, I would have started to doubt it happened myself."

"It might just have worked on someone meeker than you," Grace said. "I wonder how many times she's gotten away with that particular tactic."

As we got into my Jeep, I said, "Too many to count, most likely. One thing's certain. We can't trust a word she says to us."

"That's easy," Grace said with a laugh. "I rarely believe the people we talk to when we're investigating a case." She paused, and then added, "I wonder who this mystery book is about?"

"Funny, I was just wondering if it was even true. It almost sounded like she was trying to deflect our attention away from herself with that outlandish story. Did Lester strike you as the type who would even read a book, let alone write one?"

Grace smiled at me, and I asked, "What?"

"You don't trust much, do you?"

I shook my head. "If nothing else, I like to think that I learn from my past mistakes. Are you ready to look into this some more?"

"You know me. I'm game for anything."

As we headed back to April Springs, I couldn't help wishing that Jake were in town. We didn't often coordinate our investigations, since his work was official and mine was always under the radar, but I would have felt a lot better having him handling the case from the other side. It was wishful thinking, though. He was tied up, and Chief Martin wasn't all that likely to give me a hand with my private search. If I was going to figure out what happened to Lester Moorefield, I was going to have to do it myself.

And with a little help from my friends, too, of course.

We were almost back to April Springs when my cell phone rang. I dug it out of my pocket and said, "Hello?"

"Hey, stranger," said a voice I'd been longing to hear.

"Jake," I yelled as the wheel slipped a little in my hands. "Hang on a second."

"Pull over before you kill us both," Grace said.

I took her advice and pulled into the parking lot of an abandoned storefront for lease. "Where are you?"

"I'm still in New Bern," he admitted.

Some of the punch suddenly went out of me. "How's it going?"

I could hear his grin as he said, "We just wrapped the case up and managed to catch three bad guys, so it wasn't a bad day at all. How would you like to go out on a date with me tomorrow evening?"

"Why wait?" I asked as I glanced at my watch. "If you hurry, you can be here by seven." I couldn't believe how much I'd missed him since he'd been gone.

"I wish I could, but I've got a deskful of paperwork I have to finish first. I can leave here around noon tomorrow, though."

"That would be great." I'd never been the kind of woman who needed a man around to be happy with my life, but I had to admit that it was nice having someone close who really cared about me.

Jake said abruptly, "Sorry, I've got to go. I'll see you tomorrow."

"Bye," I said.

I hung up the phone and looked at Grace. "He's coming home tomorrow."

"I thought he was headed to April Springs," she said.

"That's what I meant." I glanced at Grace before I pulled back out into traffic. "What's that grin for?"

"It's just nice to see you so happy."

"Trust me, it feels even better than it looks."

"So, if you've got a date tomorrow, we should get busy with the rest of our day today. Any ideas on what we should do next?"

I'd been thinking about it for the past few minutes. "I want to find out more about this book, and if it even exists. Do you think Cara would know about it?"

"It's worth a shot. Do you want to call her?" Before I could say anything, she touched my arm lightly. "I mean after we get back into town."

"Let's pop by the radio station. I've got a hunch that she's probably still there."

I changed my route and headed for the radio station, but Cara's car wasn't in the parking lot.

Lester's was still there, though.

"I figured they'd have taken that in for evidence by now," Grace said.

"Maybe they've already searched it." I pulled in, an easy task now that the police tape and guard were gone.

"It's got to be a dead end."

"Not yet," I said as I parked beside it.

"What are we going to do?" Grace asked me as we got out.

"Let's see if it's unlocked."

"Suzanne, you've had some bad ideas in the past, but this one goes to the top of the list. It's one thing to have our own investigation on the side without the police, but this is a crime scene we're about to violate here."

I waved around with my hand. "Do you see any police tape anywhere?"

"No," she admitted reluctantly.

"Any cops doing any investigating?" I asked.

"No."

"Then we're okay."

I tried the driver's side door.

It was locked.

"Check the other doors," I said.

No luck. The car, if it had a single clue in it that the police had overlooked, wasn't going to do us any good.

Grace headed back toward the Jeep. "Too

bad it didn't work out coming here, but you've got to admit, that happens sometimes."

"I'm not finished yet."

I went to the building's door and tried the handle. It, too, was locked. Someone had to be there. The station couldn't run itself, could it? I pounded for a full minute.

"Give up. It's no use."

Just as I was about to take her advice, the door opened.

A young man I didn't know answered, wearing a faded blue jumpsuit with his name emblazoned on the pocket.

"Hi, Tim," I said.

His gaze narrowed. "Hello. How did you know my name?"

"I thought it was something you might want to get off your chest."

"Excuse me?"

Grace pushed past me. "Pardon my friend; she's got an odd sense of humor. She's talking about your coveralls."

He looked down and saw his own name stitched in red, then nodded his understanding.

Grace continued, "My friend was interviewed here yesterday, and she left her purse. Do you mind if we look around for it?"

"I don't know," Tim said. "I could get in trouble."

"How about a dozen free donuts tomorrow before you go to work?" I asked. In the past, donut bribes had gotten me places that even cash couldn't.

Tim looked around outside to see if anyone was watching us, and then held the door open. "Can I get them early? I go to work at six A.M."

"Perfect. I open at five-thirty."

He grinned, and then added, "Don't take anything, and don't go anywhere marked off-limits. You've got twelve minutes."

"One for each donut," I said with a smile.

He went back to his cleaning, and I started looking for Lester Moorefield's desk. I'd half expected to find it blocked off by police tape, but it was bare. I started checking drawers, but someone — most likely the police — had cleaned everything out.

"There's nothing here," I said.

Grace looked around. "Nothing that's going to help us, at any rate."

"Hang on a second, I'm not ready to give up yet."

"I have to say, you're obsessed when you get an idea in your head."

I found Tim cleaning up in the break room. He glanced at his watch. "Done so quickly? You've still got seven minutes left."

"We might not need it. Did you empty the trash can by Lester's desk today?"

He looked confused by my question. "Sure, but why do you care? Do you think someone threw it away?"

"Threw what away?" I asked.

"Your purse. That's why you're here, right?"

For an instant I'd forgotten all about our ruse. It was a good thing I wasn't a spy. I'd never be able to keep up with all the lies I'd have to tell. "That's right; my purse. It's not all that big, so it could be anywhere."

He rooted around in the collecting bin. There was a divider down the middle; one side held general trash, and the other held papers, disposable bottles, and other recyclables. "Sorry, there's no purse here."

"But you emptied Lester's can today," Grace repeated.

"I did it just before you two came in, but it was mostly just paper. I'd have noticed a purse."

I nodded, and made an urgent gesture to Grace that I hoped Tim wouldn't see. She caught on without any more coaching. "Tim, is there supposed to be water leaking in the bathroom in the hallway?"

"I thought they fixed that," he said as he

grabbed a mop from his cart and sped for the hall.

The second he was gone, I said, "That was an oddly freaky good guess."

"Don't give me too much credit. There was a SLIPPERY FLOOR sign there when we walked in, and a mop was leaning up against the wall."

"That was still fast thinking on your part."

"Save the compliments for later," Grace said. "You hunt. I'll keep watch."

I wasn't about to argue. She'd bought me some time, no matter how brief it might be, and I couldn't squander it. I started looking through the papers on top of the recycling section. A few sheets had Lester's name on them with his chicken-scratch handwriting, so I scooped them up first.

Grace hissed, "Hurry."

There was no time to be selective. I grabbed everything I could and stuffed it all under my T-shirt. If I held my arms against my stomach, I might get out of there without leaving a paper trail behind me.

"There's no leak," Tim said as soon as he returned.

"It must have been my imagination. Sorry," Grace said.

He looked at me as I clutched my stomach. "You okay?"

"I think I had a bad egg salad sandwich for lunch today," I said.

I could see the displeasure on his face, most likely not from my illness, but from the prospect that he'd be the one who'd have to clean it up.

I made a small moaning noise, and then I said, "If you don't mind, we'd better go."

He looked downright relieved as I stumbled out clutching my stomach.

"When did you have egg salad?" Grace asked when we were in the parking lot again.

"A few weeks ago."

"And it's just bothering you now?"

"No, but how else could I explain holding my hands against my stomach like I was cramping up?" I lifted one corner of my shirt and showed her the papers I'd managed to sneak out of the building. Maybe something there would give us a clue about who would want Lester dead. No, that wasn't right. There were plenty of "whos" already. What I really needed was a way to narrow things down.

I held my T-shirt out and shoved the papers in the backseat of the Jeep. "Let's get out of here, shall we?"

"You read my mind," she said.

We drove away, and I asked, "Where should we go now? We can't walk into the

Boxcar Grill and start digging through those papers; it would be too easy for someone to see what we were up to. The donut shop's out. I know these were all recycled, but I can't help feeling they're trash, and I don't want them there. If we take them to my house, Momma's going to want to know what we're up to, and I don't want to have that particular conversation, do you?"

"Let's take them to my place," Grace volunteered.

"It's our best option, isn't it? Are you sure you don't have to get back to work now?"

"I've got a confession to make," Grace said with a smile. "I get three discretionary days a month as a supervisor, and I'm using them right now, all in a row."

"You sure you want to burn them helping me?"

"Until Johnny Depp comes to his senses and sweeps me off my feet, I can't think of a better use of my time."

I laughed. "You've got a pass, then. If Mr. Depp shows up, you're off the hook, with my blessing."

"Whether I have it or not, you can bet that I'm going to take advantage of the opportunity if it ever comes up."

"I don't blame you a bit."

We got to Grace's place and started going

107

through the papers on her broad porch. As we searched for something relevant to our investigation, Grace said softly, "I envy you, Suzanne."

I looked up and asked, "Because of my looks, my charm, or my general disposition?"

She laughed. "All of those, actually, but also because you have Jake in your life. It's been so long since I've dated a decent man I bet I've forgotten how."

"I'm sure it will come back to you. How long has your dry spell lasted? I bet it's at least two weeks since you went out with anyone."

"That wasn't a real date. It was dinner with Kyle Farrar, and I nearly fell asleep halfway through the appetizers. That man could bore the fleas off a dog."

"He picked you up, fed you, and brought you back home. That's a date in my book."

"I still don't think it counts, but even if it did, do you know how many second or third dates I've been on in the past two years?"

I tried to think of all the men Grace had dated in the past, and while I knew there'd been a healthy number of potential suitors, she hadn't really connected with anyone in quite some time. "I didn't realize," I said.

"I'm sorry if I keep throwing Jake in your face."

"That's not what I meant," she said. "All I'm saying is that it must be nice to be you right now."

"Besides the whole murder-pointing-to-me situation, you mean?"

"Besides that," she acknowledged with a slight smile.

"It would be even better if Jake lived here in April Springs."

"Be careful what you wish for," Grace said as she continued to scan her share of the papers we'd retrieved. "If he moved to town, you might get sick of him, seeing him all the time."

"I'll take that chance," I said.

"But do you think he ever will?" Grace asked.

At least a part of my mind heard her. The other segment was focused on the document I'd just pulled out of the stack.

We might have just caught a break in finding out who killed Lester Moorefield, if the clue in my hand meant what I thought it did.

# APPLE FRITTERS

These fritters are delightful, especially when they've had a chance to cool a little. We have them with a touch of powdered sugar, but some folks like to add a little apple butter for a double whammy!

## Ingredients

3/4 cup all purpose flour
1/4 cup sugar (white)
1 tablespoon baking powder
1 tablespoon cinnamon
1/3 cup milk (2% or whole)
1/4 teaspoon salt
1 egg, beaten
1/2 cup chopped apple (something tart; I like Granny Smiths for this)

## Directions

Heat canola oil for frying to 360 degrees while you mix the batter. Sift the dry ingredients, then stir in milk and beaten egg. Fold in chopped apple, and then take a teaspoon of batter and rake it into the fryer with another spoon. If the dough doesn't rise soon, gently nudge it with a chopstick, being careful not to splatter oil. After two minutes, check, and then flip, frying for another minute on the other side. These times may vary given too many factors to count, so keep a close eye on the fritters.

Makes about a dozen small fritters.

# CHAPTER 6

"What did you find, Suzanne?"

"What makes you think I uncovered any-thing?" I asked as I continued staring at the paper in my hand.

"I know you better than that. You look as though you've just been slapped."

"Take a look at this," I said as I handed her the paper I'd found. The document itself had been an internal memo about the station's next on-air promotion, but it was what Lester had written on the side that had caught my attention.

"Be careful digging into Lacy Newman's history. Don't turn your back on her, and never forget that no matter how sweet she might look, she's a killer. If she's done it once, she can do it again."

The paper nearly fluttered out of Grace's hand to the floor. "He finally lost his mind, didn't he?"

"What do you mean?"

Grace looked at me as if I were the one who'd slipped out of my ties to reality. "We're talking about Lacy Newman, the same woman who volunteers with the Scouts and cooks at the soup kitchen when she's not working? Do you honestly think under any circumstances that she could be a killer?"

"I don't know," I said. Everything Grace said was true. I knew Lacy pretty well. We'd been assigned as a team in the park cleanup sweep the year before, and I'd found her charming, funny, and the least likely person I'd ever met in my life to be a killer. "Why would he just make this up?"

"You knew Lester. He loved fabricating stories to get people's attention."

"He did, I know," I said as I took the paper from her hand, "but you've got to admit that no matter how much he embellished what he said, there was always a kernel of truth in it."

She frowned at me. "So, donuts really are killers."

"If you eat too much of any treat it's going to have a bad result on your health," I said. "Don't put me in the position of defending Lester, because I can't bring myself to do it. All I'm saying is that there's a chance there's more than just smoke here."

"Wow, we have quite a list of suspects, don't we?" Grace asked.

"Do you have some paper and a pen?" I asked her. "We need to sort things out."

She said, "Not out here, but I have something we can use inside."

I nodded. "Then I suggest we move this inside."

Once we were in her living room, Grace reached into the drawer of a nearby table and pulled out a tablet and a mechanical pencil. "Will this do?"

"Perfectly. Let's see, who do we have so far on our suspect list?"

As we discussed the case, I wrote down the names. In the end, we included: Lacy Newman; Cam Hamilton, the mayor; Nancy Patton, Lester's ex; Sherry Lance, our only town councilwoman; an unnamed builder from Hudson Creek who had also been maligned by Lester; and Cara, his segment producer.

"I still don't think we should put Cara's name on the list," I said.

"Come on, can you imagine working with that blowhard day in and day out and not wanting to spike his coffee with battery acid?"

"He was strangled, remember," I said.

"Even better."

I thought about it, and then said, "Okay, she stays in. Wow, this is going to be a logistical nightmare, isn't it? Grace, we are going to need to talk with an awful lot of people."

"Then we should get started," she said.

"I agree, but who do we speak with first? We know most of the people on this list. We can't really keep using our article cover story to get them to talk to us."

She shrugged. "We don't have to. The ones we can't bribe with donuts, we ask outright."

"I didn't think you approved of that style of inquiry."

"What can I say? It seems to be working this time. I'm willing to keep doing it if you are."

"Then it's simple enough; when all else fails, we tell the truth," I said with a grin.

There was a pounding at the front door, and I asked Grace, "Are you expecting anyone?"

She frowned. "Not that I can think of."

We walked to the door together, and when Grace opened it, we found George standing there. "Sorry about that, but I couldn't find your doorbell."

Grace stepped outside and pointed to a button that had been painted several times over the years. "It's right there."

"You can't see it," George protested.

"That's okay. I don't really like having visitors, anyway," she answered with a smile.

I knew Grace could go on for days like that, but George wasn't that playful on his best day, and this had clearly not been one of those.

He dismissed her and looked at me. "Got a second?"

"How'd you know I'd be here?"

As we all stepped inside, he asked, "Where else would you be? Besides, I saw your Jeep in the driveway."

"You could have always called me," I said.

"I did. There wasn't an answer. Check your cell phone."

I pulled it out of my pocket, expecting to see that the battery had died again. I was constantly having trouble getting the thing to take a charge, but the display lit up when I opened it. "It's working just fine. It must be your phone."

George pulled his cell out and hit a number speed dial. As he held it to his ear, he said, "I don't know what's going on, but it's not ringing on my end."

I looked at my phone and finally noticed

that I'd accidently turned the ringer off. There was a button on the side to turn it off and on, and it seemed to be getting activated more often lately when I had it in my pocket. Maybe I'd better cut back on my own donut consumption if it was tightening my jeans that much. The next thing I knew, my pants would be calling Switzerland, and I didn't think I could afford the phone bills.

"Sorry about that."

"Don't apologize. In all honesty, I'm relieved. I thought I was going crazy."

Grace smiled at him. "I think it's sweet you have Suzanne on your speed dial."

George shrugged. "As often as she's in trouble, it's a good number to have on hand."

"I'd like to deny it," I said, "but I can't, since it's true. What's up?"

"I finally found out something about Lester," he said.

"Is it about his wife?" Grace asked. I'd wanted George to be able to tell us about Nancy, if that was his information, but my friend had just ruined the opportunity for him. Having his contacts with the police department cut off had to hurt him on more than just an investigating level.

"He's married?" George asked with a

frown. "I didn't come across that yet."

"That's why there are three of us," I said. I shot Grace a warning look, which she finally saw. "What did you find out?"

"Lester went to prison fifteen years ago," George said.

"Did he kill someone?" I blurted out.

George looked surprised by the question. "No, it was some kind of fraud. Lester was an investment broker, and he embezzled funds from a handful of clients. By the time he got caught, most of the money was gone, and he only made partial restitution. From what I heard, when he got out of jail, the only job he could get was at a radio station sweeping floors. He started moving around, and finally worked his way into a time slot here in town."

"How much money are we talking about here?" I asked.

George flipped through his notebook, the same type he'd used when he'd been a cop, he'd told me once. "Two point seven million dollars," he answered. "They only found a hundred grand of it when they finally figured out what he was up to."

"Is there a chance he still had any of it when he was murdered?" That much money could provide two more motives for his murder, by a former client, or another thief

118

looking for a big payday.

George clearly didn't believe that. "Have you seen the way he lived? I sincerely doubt he had more than a couple hundred dollars to his name when he died."

"It's something to keep in mind as we're digging," I said. I suddenly remembered watching Lester eat once, covering his food with both arms. It had struck me as odd, and now I realized that it must have been prison etiquette, keeping others from stealing from his tray. How did I not know this about Lester? We all lived in a small town. Then again, some folks were better at keeping secrets than others. I got out our list and added two more categories to it: investors and thieves.

George looked interested. "What have you got there?"

"It's what we've found out so far," I said as I handed him the list, "and what we suspect."

After we explained what we'd uncovered, George asked, "Should we split this up, or tackle them all together?"

"I'm not sure what's the best way to handle it," I said.

He tapped the list with his index finger for a minute or two, and then said, "You two should work as one team, and I'll work as the other."

"That's not much of a team you'll have there," Grace said.

"That's okay. I can handle myself if there's trouble."

"What about us?" Grace asked with a smile.

"I figure you two could talk your way out of just about any situation, so I'm not all that worried about you. Let's divide it up this way. I'll take the crooks who might want to rip him off and the investors he bilked, and you two take the politicians. The rest we'll get to when we're through with the first round. How does that sound?"

"Like a good plan to me," I said.

He nodded. "Good. Let's say we meet at the donut shop tomorrow at noon and compare notes."

"Thanks for your help, George."

He tipped a finger toward me as though he were touching the brim of a hat. "Glad to be of service."

After he was gone, Grace said, "He really loves doing this, doesn't he?"

"It can't be because of the pay. All the donuts you can eat is not exactly a living wage, is it?"

Grace laughed. "Your donuts are good, but they're not that good. So, should we get busy ourselves?"

"I'm game if you are. Who would you like to tackle first, Mayor Hamilton, or Councilwoman Lance?"

"Let's go to city hall and see if either one of them is in," Grace said.

"I'm ready if you are."

Since running our small town wasn't a full-time job for anyone, it was often difficult catching anyone in city hall except Polly North, a retired school librarian who worked the desk as a volunteer. Polly was petite, barely weighing ninety pounds soaking wet, but there was something about her that made people listen whenever she spoke. To cross her was either brave or foolhardy, and no one escaped unscathed from her wrath.

"Hey Polly," I said the second I saw her. It had been a hard habit to break, not calling her Mrs. North, as just about half the town had called her at one point in their lives, but she was insistent, and Polly usually got what she wanted.

"Well, goodness me. It's the twin sisters from different mothers," she said as she looked up from her crossword puzzle. "You two always were thick as thieves. You've never given up that bond, have you?"

121

"Are you surprised by that?" Grace asked her.

"With some I would be, but not you two. What brings you to city hall? I'm sure you're not here just to brighten my day."

"Hey, if we can kill two birds," Grace said.

"I always disliked that saying," Polly said, her disapproval evident in her expression. "Who on earth would want to kill one bird, let alone two? It's a dreadful commentary on the human race that it's in the common vernacular, don't you think?"

"I've never cared for it myself," I said with a smile, more for Grace than Polly.

My "twin" stuck her tongue out at me, and Polly caught it. Her laughter rang through the empty hallway. "Enough foolishness. What can I do for you?"

"We're looking for Cam Hamilton and Sherry Lance. Any chance either one of them is hanging around?"

Polly shook her head. "The mayor is in Charlotte for a meeting, and the councilwoman is most likely at her regular job."

"So we can catch her there," I said.

"You can always try," Polly replied, "but I wouldn't count on it. She spends more time in the field than you could imagine."

"We'll take our chances," I said.

"It was good seeing you," Grace added.

Polly grinned at us both. "And why shouldn't it be?"

We were both laughing as we left city hall.

Unfortunately, when we got to Sherry's veterinary office, she was out on a call, and her receptionist wasn't all that eager to tell us where she was.

It appeared that we'd hit a brick wall, at least for the moment.

I felt my stomach rumbling, and Grace must have heard it. "That pasta was wonderful, but it didn't really stick, did it?"

I glanced at my watch. "If I know my mother, she's ready to put dinner on the table. Care to join us?"

"I'd love to, but I have some paperwork at home I have to catch up on."

"I thought you were taking a few days off," I said.

"I am, but if I don't do this, it will be hanging over my head until I go back. It's tough being a supervisor sometimes."

"But look at the perks."

After I dropped Grace off, I headed home. It had been a long day, and I was looking forward to a home-cooked meal. Living with my mother since my divorce had definitely had its share of downsides, but one of the strongest positives was that I got to eat some of the best meals in town just for the cost of doing dishes.

It almost made everything else I had to put up with worthwhile.

Almost.

"Hi, Momma," I said as I walked into the kitchen of our place. Our cottage might not be grand by most people's standards, but what it lacked in size it made up for in character. There were beautiful built-in cabinets everywhere, and lots of wood trim that glowed with lustrous coats of varnish. I was thankful for everyone in my family who had lived there that no one had ever decided to paint the wood. The house's location was another reason I loved living there. We were on the edge of a lovely park, and growing up, I'd been a special kid with her very own playground just outside her front door.

My mother frowned as she saw me. Instead of a standard greeting, she asked, "Suzanne, you're at it again, aren't you?"

"That depends. I have to know what you're talking about before I confess to doing anything wrong. Fool me once, shame on you, and all of that."

"You know full well that I'm referring to Lester Moorefield," she said.

"What about him?" I was going to keep playing dumb as long as I could, and I was willing to keep stringing her along all night if she was game.

"You are investigating his murder on your own, aren't you?"

"What makes you say that?"

She shook her head slightly. "Stop it," she said, the agitation clear in her voice. "I won't play games with you. Answer me."

I didn't want to, but after thirty seconds, I couldn't take the silence anymore. "Somebody's got to figure out who killed Lester. I don't want anyone in town believing that I'm a murderer."

"Has anyone said anything to you?" It was clear that my mother had gone from disappointed to angry to protecting her chick, all in a split second. She was allowed to criticize me all she wanted, but if someone else said one disparaging word, my mother would go for the throat.

"Not that I've heard," I admitted softly, touched by her reaction, "but can you possibly imagine that the rumors aren't already flying around town? Let's face it, everyone has a reason to be suspicious. I had an argument with the man and the next day he was found with one of my pastries jammed down his throat, even if that wasn't what killed him. It's not exactly a leap of reasoning for folks to think I might have had something to do with it."

"Those who know you won't even consider the possibility that you are a murderer," she said.

"I appreciate you saying it, even if it's not true." I was tired of thinking about Lester Moorefield for one day. "How was your day?"

"Busy," she said.

When more details weren't offered, I decided to drop it. My mother had her hand in several businesses, and she mostly liked to keep that part of her life separate from mine. We'd forged a sometimes-uneasy alliance when I'd moved back home, and it didn't hurt either one of us to have a few secrets of our own. "At least you're not bored. Any thoughts on dinner?"

She looked at the clock. "It's taken care of. We should be eating in ten minutes."

I sniffed the air, and I picked up the unmistakable scent of her homemade cornbread. Growing up, I'd had cornbread in the school cafeteria, but it was nothing like Momma's. Where theirs had been coarse and flat, my mother's was light and just a little bit sweet. I wasn't sure how most Southerners would react to it, but it was a little bit of heaven to me. "Brown beans, chopped scallions, and spinach, too?"

126

"I thought it would be a nice change of pace," she said.

"I agree." Unlike many of my peers, I'd always been a huge fan of spinach growing up, and I loved the combination we were having. It had to be in the top ten of my comfort foods, and that was saying a lot. At times I wondered if too much of my comfort was derived from what I ate, but wasn't that true of just about all of us?

Momma and I sat down and enjoyed a hearty meal, and I was happy again to be living where I was. Real butter melted into the muffins, dripping slightly onto my fingertips. "That was delicious," I said as I ate the last cornbread muffin bud. While some folks served theirs in huge square slabs, my mother had a pan that produced perfect little cornbread muffins. "Tell you what. That was so great, I'll do dishes tonight."

"Thank you, but I don't mind. I'll do them," she said. "I know you've been under a great deal of stress today. Why don't you take a walk in the park, and when you come back, I'll have an apple crisp pie out of the oven."

I looked at the calendar, and when Momma noticed, she asked, "What are you looking for?"

"I was just checking to see if it was my birthday."

She laughed. "Can't a mother pamper her daughter on occasion for no reason in particular?"

I hugged her, and even though I was a good five inches taller than she was, I still felt very much her little girl. "You have my permission, even my blessing, to spoil me any time you want to," I said.

When I pulled away, she was smiling gently at me. "Now go walk and leave me to those dishes."

"Yes, ma'am," I said. I grabbed a light jacket on the way out, just in case things had cooled off any since I'd come in. Sure enough, the temperature had been dropping, and there was a chill in the air. It was as if each day were divided into two different seasons, one of the reasons it was close to my favorite time of year. I pulled the edges of my jacket close, and then walked the loop around the park. There were several spots that were significant to me, from where I'd learned to ride my bike, to where I'd had my first kiss, and even where I'd sat and cried three weeks later when that same boy broke my heart. As I always did, I touched the bark of the Patriot's Tree as I passed it by, an old oak that had a murderous past. It was there that British soldiers had been hanged, and then nearly a hundred years later, Yankee spies had joined them in making history. A weathered plaque below it said, in Thomas Jefferson's words, "The tree of liberty must be refreshed from time to time with the blood of patriots and tyrants." It seemed that my forefathers had taken the quote literally.

I finished my loop, and was nearing the cottage when I saw someone silhouetted on the porch. As I got closer, I couldn't believe who was standing there.

# CHAPTER 7

"Jake! You came early." I wrapped my arms around him, and he twirled me in the air. After we kissed, I pulled back. "I didn't think you were coming until tomorrow."

"What can I say? I missed you too much to stay away. I figured I could do my paperwork here just as easily as I could there, so why not be with you? You're okay with me coming early, aren't you?"

"Are you kidding? You never need my permission to come here," I said.

Jake hugged me. "It's been too long."

"I missed you, too. Have you had dinner yet? Momma made brown beans and cornbread. I'm sure there's enough left to put a plate together for you."

"Thanks, but I ate on the way," he said.

I laughed. "Trust me, if you're the least bit hungry, it's worth tasting. You've never had anything like it. I guarantee it."

"It's tempting, but I really am full," he

protested.

The porch light flipped on, and Momma walked out and joined us. "I thought I heard voices," she said. "Jake, it's wonderful to see you."

"You, too, Mrs. Hart."

"Please, I told you to call me Dorothy."

"You can tell me all you want, but that won't make me do it," he said with a smile.

"Would you do it for a piece of apple pie fresh out of the oven?" Momma asked him.

He didn't even need to think about it. "Sold. For a piece of your pie, I'll call you the Queen of England, if you'd like."

"What's my name, then?"

"Dorothy," he said. Jake Bishop was definitely old-school, and I knew how hard that concession must have been for him to make.

"Don't make him jump through any more hoops, Momma," I said. "Besides, he just told me he's full."

"Speak for yourself, woman," Jake said with a smile. "I've suddenly got all of the room I need."

"Pie is served in the main dining hall, then," my mother said, and we all went in and enjoyed a piece of her warm apple-crisp pie. Her recipe, a closely guarded family secret, was known throughout four coun-

131

ties, and it always drew the highest bidder whenever she baked one for a charity auction.

When we were finished, Momma started collecting the dishes, and Jake and I rose to help.

"You two go out and enjoy our lovely weather. I'll take care of this."

"Thanks," I said as I kissed my mother's cheek. She knew how much I'd missed Jake, and she was doing everything she could to give us both some privacy.

"Mrs. . . . Dorothy, that was delicious," Jake said.

My mother laughed robustly. "I'm not sure how I feel about you calling me Mrs. Dorothy, but I suppose it's a start. Good night, Jake."

"Good night, ma'am."

Jake and I walked out on the porch and took our places on the porch swing. I'd done the exact same thing with half a dozen boyfriends over the years, including my ex, Max, but none had been as special to me as this one at this exact moment in time. Jake and I had something that Max and I had never shared; we were close in ways that didn't require the tumultuous highs and lows that I used to believe true love required. There was a great deal to be said for the steadying feeling of being loved and protected, no matter what.

I reached out and held Jake's hand in silent appreciation, happy that we'd been able to come this far in our relationship. We'd encountered some rough patches getting there, and I didn't doubt that more would come, but it had all been worth it.

"So, what's new with you?" Jake asked as we swung gently on the swing.

I hadn't said anything about Lester Moorefield yet, not wanting to ruin the evening. "I just want to enjoy tonight. Can we talk about things tomorrow?"

The chair suddenly stopped swinging. "Suzanne, I don't like the sound of that."

"It's nothing. Not really. Well, almost nothing."

He let go of my hand and looked at me. "That's not much of an answer, even by your standards. What happened?"

"There was a murder last night," I finally admitted.

Jake's smile was completely gone now. "Tell me you weren't involved."

"I wasn't involved," I answered.

"Now tell me the truth."

"I was involved."

Jake let out a breath of air, and then said, "Let's hear it."

I knew this moment of joy had been too good to last. "You've heard of Lester Moorefield, right?"

"We met once. He's the guy with the radio show, right?"

"Was. Someone murdered him last night."

That piqued Jake's interest. "How exactly were you involved with that?"

I bit my lip, and then decided I might as well tell him everything. He'd get it out of me eventually. Jake was too good a cop to just drop it. "Lester broadcast an editorial about the evils of donuts, so naturally I had to have a conversation with him about it after I heard it."

Jake looked off into the park for a few moments before he spoke again. "And by conversation, you mean confrontation."

"I may have raised my voice once or twice, but what he said on the radio was pretty inflammatory. He called my donuts poison."

"Don't tell me that's how he died."

"No, there wasn't any poison used," I answered.

"At least there's that," Jake said.

"He was strangled, and then someone shoved one of my éclairs down his throat to make their point. It wasn't pretty."

Jake stood, walked to the edge of the porch, and gazed out into the darkness of the park. "Suzanne, how do you keep managing to get yourself in trouble like this?"

"It's a gift, I guess. This wasn't my fault, Jake. I didn't do it, and it was news to me when the chief sent for me this morning. Now, can we talk about something else and pretend this never happened?"

"I'm not sure that I can," he said.

I patted the seat beside me. "You can at least try."

He shrugged, and then took his seat again. "I suppose this makes my next question a moot one."

"Who knows? I might surprise you. Go ahead and ask."

"Any chance you can take a few days off? I've got some vacation time coming, and I thought we might go to Gatlinburg together. There's a place on a stream I heard about while I was away that sounds perfect."

I loved Gatlinburg, Tennessee. There was a chair lift that climbed the mountain that I could ride all day, and they had an aquarium that was one of the best I'd ever been to. I wouldn't go near the tourist town in the summer, but when the kids were in school, it was a wonderful place to be. I'd shared my fond memories of the place with Jake once. "It's a sweet thought, but you know I can't get away."

"Suzanne, everyone deserves a vacation, even us. I could book us there in a heartbeat. All you have to do is say yes."

"If it were any other time I'd be tempted, but I can't do it, Jake. I'm sorry." I kissed him, and then added, "It's a sweet thought, though."

"That's what I figured, but I wanted to go ahead and ask anyway. Besides Lester, is there anything else going on around here?"

I'd just about forgotten the juiciest tidbit I'd picked up lately. "Chief Martin's getting a divorce," I said.

"It happens, and more times to cops than most people realize."

"He told my mother about it first thing. He's had a crush on her most of his life, and it appears he's finally doing something about it."

"How does she feel about that?"

"She's not happy about his intentions," I said. "Just between us, I don't think the chief has a chance."

Jake studied me for a moment, and then asked, "Why do you sound so happy when you say that, Suzanne?"

"I didn't mean to, but come on; it's no secret that he's not my favorite person in the world. Could you imagine him coming around here courting my mother? I'm not sure I could take that, even though I told her that she had my blessing."

"Does your blessing really matter, though? She needs to do what's right for her."

I turned to look at him. "What do you mean?"

"Doesn't your mother deserve another chance at happiness? We can love more than one person in our lives."

That reference was to him, not my mother. Jake had lost his wife in a car accident, and his continuing devotion to her had been a major stumbling block for us at first. "I told her the exact same thing. Jake, I have no problem with her dating," I said. "I'm just not so sure I'm crazy about the idea of her dating him."

I caught a glimpse of Jake, and saw that he was smiling.

"What's so amusing?"

"Children aren't allowed to choose who their parents go out with any more than parents can choose their children's dates."

"I suppose you're right," I said. "Ultimately she'll do whatever she wants, but I'm still not giving the chief much of a chance."

"Just don't try to worsen his odds even more," Jake said.

"I won't do that," I promised halfheartedly. "As a matter of fact, I'm planning to stay out of it completely." I started to yawn, but caught it just in time. At least I thought I had.

Jake stood and stretched, and then said, "I just had a long drive, and it's getting late. I'd better call it a night."

I glanced at my watch. "It's only eight-thirty."

"And a good half hour past your bedtime at that. Don't worry, we'll have time to catch up more tomorrow."

"Sometimes my working hours are a real curse," I said as I stood.

"Don't worry, it isn't enough to drive me off."

He wrapped me in his arms, and I breathed him in deeply. Not only did I feel safe and warm in his arms, I felt needed, wanted, and loved. It was almost as though we drew energy off each other in moments like this, and I was so glad he'd found his way into my life, and had allowed me to come into his.

"I'll see you tomorrow," he said, after giving me one final good night kiss.

"Bright and early?" I asked.

"For me, not you. I should be by the donut shop around noon."

"Coward." I laughed at him.

"I like to think of myself as wise. Even if you're not on vacation, I am. If I don't take these days, I'll lose them. I'm going to sleep in, and then try my best not to do anything productive for the next few days."

"That sounds like a fine plan to me," I said.

"Trust me, I get enough excitement on my day job. Vacation is a time for me to recharge, and I'm in bad need of it at the moment."

"I just wish I could join you. I honestly do."

"That makes two of us. Don't worry, there will be other times for us, Suzanne. See you tomorrow."

I waved to him, and stood on the porch until he was gone.

At least Jake hadn't volunteered to help me find Lester's killer during his time off. I had no desire to drag him into this. He got enough murder and mayhem in his job, and I didn't want it to ruin one of his rare vacation days.

When I walked back inside, Momma was still up. "How nice to have company. Jake looked delighted to see you," she said as she glanced up from the crossword puzzle she was doing.

"Believe me, it was mutual," I said.

"Of course it was. Will he be able to stay long this time?"

"He's taking a few days off," I admitted.

"You should, too," Momma said.

"That's what he said, but you know my schedule. I just can't."

She pointed her pencil at me. "You deserve a vacation. If you can't get anyone else to help out at the donut shop, close it for a few days. Folks can live without your confections for that long."

"I can't afford to," I said as I started up the stairs.

"Then I'll work there."

I smiled at her. "I never knew you made donuts," I said.

"There are a great many things you don't know about me."

"I appreciate the offer, but I need to be there."

She frowned at me. "Suzanne, if you are worried about the money, then I'll cover your losses. There's more to life than working all of the time."

I knew my mother was serious if she was willing to spend that much. "I couldn't take your money. Besides, I can't leave for more reasons than that."

"What's stopping you?"

I left the stairs and walked back to her.

"Why is this suddenly so important to you? I don't get it."

"I want you to be happy."

"Funny, I want the exact same thing for you," I said. "Tell you what. You go out on a real date, and I'll take you up on your vacation offer."

She shook her head. "My proposal to you isn't contingent on anything else, and yours shouldn't be, either. Take it or don't take it; I won't allow you to manipulate me like that."

"I meant what I said," I replied as I softened my voice. "I honestly do want you to find some happiness again."

"You sound a great deal like Phillip Martin."

It was all I could do not to roll my eyes. "He's not my first choice of suitors, that shouldn't come as a surprise to anyone, but if you want to see him, or anyone else, you know you have my blessing."

She put her puzzle down on the couch. "Suddenly I've completely lost interest in this conversation."

"And just when it was getting interesting," I said with a smile.

"You're not fooling anyone, Suzanne. The real reason you won't take time off is that you're investigating Lester Moorefield's murder on your own, and you're afraid if you go away, you'll miss something. Don't try to deny it, I know you too well."

"I wasn't about to deny anything," I replied. "I can't have that cloud of suspicion hanging over my head. It could ruin my business, and my life in April Springs, and we both know it."

"You should let the police handle it."

I shook my head, and there was no way I could keep the sarcasm out of my voice. "Yeah, because that's worked out so well for me in the past."

"Suzanne, you're just trying to be difficult now."

"I don't have to try very hard, though, do I?" I was suddenly exhausted by our verbal sparring. I walked back, leaned over, and kissed her on the forehead. "Good night. I love you."

"I love you, too," she said.

I was nearly up the stairs when I heard her add, "Sweet dreams."

It didn't take long for me to fall asleep. Working at the donut shop and then adding too much drama to the rest of my day was exhausting. I went to sleep and tried to put everything out of my mind. Amazingly enough, I was able to, and when I woke up the next morning, I was ready to take on the world. I needed to make some progress in my investigation before my reputation took a hit it couldn't recover from.

By ten, we'd done good business at Donut Hearts, but I could tell some of our regulars were clearly avoiding us. It didn't take much to turn the ink on my books from black to red, and I promised myself I'd redouble my efforts to clear my name.

I was standing by the door watching cars drive past us without stopping in, and I wondered where everyone was going in such a hurry. As I glanced down the street, I saw the fellow in the clown outfit walking toward the donut shop again. As soon as he approached the door, I slid the lock in place and flipped the sign to CLOSED. It was probably a little crueler than I needed to be, but he got my message. His head dropped a little, and then I saw him walk up the tracks toward the Boxcar Grill. The overshoes he wore flapped in the grass as he walked away, and I decided that it wasn't fair to take my problems with clowns out on him. I resolved to do a little better the next time, if he ever showed up again.

I was still watching him when I saw someone else approach the shop. It was Councilwoman Sherry Lance, and she looked confused by my CLOSED sign. I flipped it over and unlocked the door just in time. Sherry was tall and lean, with a short ponytail, piercing green eyes, and a ruddy complexion.

"Are you closing?" she asked me as I opened the door for her.

"No," I said simply. I would have loved to give her some kind of clever explanation, and I would probably think of one in a few hours, but for the moment, my mind was drawing a blank.

She frowned at my lack of embellishment. "I heard you wanted to see me."

"It can wait, if you'd like," I said. "Why don't you come on in and have a donut on the house?"

Sherry frowned and shook her head as she glanced at her watch. "I have five minutes right now, and I can't promise that again for the rest of the day."

"Wow, you must be busy."

"Between my practice and town business, I've got a full schedule."

I decided to make my offer again. It was amazing how much it loosened some people up to get a free donut. "Are you sure you wouldn't like a donut and coffee while we talk?"

She shook her head. "No, thanks. If you

don't mind, could we speak outside?"

Sherry acted as though the mere presence of donuts was offensive to her. I knew some folks believed that there was nothing redeeming about what I created, but it always amazed me how adamant they were that no one else should enjoy things they considered bad, either.

"Emma, grab the front," I called out. "Back in five."

I left the shop, and Sherry and I took an empty table outside. The second she sat, she asked, "What can I do for you?"

"It's about Lester Moorefield," I said. "I heard you two didn't get along."

Sherry's chin dipped. "Now where on earth would you hear something like that?"

"I can't divulge my sources," I said, "but I understand it's common knowledge. He came after you with one of his editorials recently, didn't he?"

Sherry laughed. "Is that what this is about? Lester had a habit of stirring up trouble. Suzanne, you should know that better than anyone."

"What did he say about you?"

"I don't really want to repeat it," Sherry said. One hand adjusted her ponytail, and I wondered if it was some kind of nervous tic of hers.

"I can get Cara to run the tape for me, but wouldn't it just be easier if you told me yourself?"

Sherry seemed to think about that, and then said, "I don't see what harm it could do. I had the unpleasant task of putting down his sister's dog last week. Her little dachshund had cancer, and the only thing she knew was pain. Ending that dog's misery was the only humane thing to do, but Lester was outraged. He called me a killer on the air."

"I bet that made you angry."

"Don't put words in my mouth, Suzanne. The only way to handle a bully sometimes is to push back. I had my attorney send him a letter to cease and desist the attacks on my practice, and Lester shut right up. Does that sound like I was mad enough to murder him? I don't treat people, just animals. While it's true they can't tell me where it hurts, they also lack the basic ability to be cruel intentionally, and I'll take that trade-off seven days a week."

Sherry was quite calm about the whole thing; too calm, perhaps. "Does the mayor feel the same way you do?"

"About Lester? Honestly, do you think for one second that you can find anyone who actually liked the man? I'm sure Cam had his own issues with him, but if you want anything more than that, you'll have to speak directly with him."

She had all the right answers.

Evidently our interview was over. As she stood, I said, "Thanks for coming by. By the way, the offer still stands. I'd love to treat you to a donut, any time."

The look of distaste on her face was clear. "No, I don't think so. No."

As she walked up the street, I reflected that there was something about the woman I didn't trust. Her answers were too carefully supplied, as though she were reading them from a script. Then again, she could have been completely on the level with me.

If I was being honest about it, I had to admit that there was just something about a person who didn't like donuts that bothered me.

Would she have used a donut to kill Lester? She might, if she hated them as much as she had him. It could have been a symbolic way of ridding herself of two enemies at once.

But could I see Sherry having that much passion about anything?

I wasn't sure. I'd been fooled before, and I wasn't about to jump to any conclusions just yet.

# POTATO-BASED DONUTS

You'd never know there's any potato in this recipe unless you watch it being made. The donuts it produces are crispy, delicious, and hold their taste well. Some folks make them around the holidays, but we like them any time of year!

## Ingredients

1 cup mashed potato (medium baking potato, peeled and cooked, then cooled)
2 tablespoons butter
1 cup sugar (white)
1 egg, beaten
3/4 cup milk (2% or whole)
2 cups all purpose flour
1 tablespoon baking powder

## Directions

Heat canola oil to 360 degrees while you mix the batter. Take your cooled mashed potato and add butter to it, mixing thoroughly. Then slowly add the sugar, the beaten egg, and the milk. Mix, then in a separate bowl sift the flour and baking powder together. Add the dry ingredients to the wet, stirring as you go. When the oil reaches its proper temperature, take a teaspoon of batter and rake it into the fryer with another spoon. If the dough doesn't rise soon, gently nudge it with a chopstick, being careful not to splatter oil. After two minutes, check, and then flip, frying for another minute on the other side. These times may vary given too many factors to count, so keep a close eye on the donuts.

Makes around a dozen small drop donuts.

# CHAPTER 8

"Perfect timing," I told Grace as she walked in at a few minutes till noon, closing time at Donut Hearts. Jake still hadn't shown up. How could anyone possibly stay in bed until that late in the day?

"I wasn't sure what we'd be doing today, so I slept in," she said with a smile that faded as she looked at the packed display cases behind me. "You didn't have a good day, did you?"

"Not even a little bit," I said. I wasn't sure how it could possibly be Sherry's fault, but I hadn't had more than three customers after she'd come by. Or had it been the clown? Could it possibly have been bad karma turning him away? I wasn't entirely certain I believed in that, but I wasn't going to take any chances the next time. He'd get a feast, as long as he could afford to pay for it. On a more pragmatic level, I couldn't afford to turn anyone away, given the poor flow of customers.

"What are you going to do with all of them?" she asked.

"I thought I'd give them to the church. Tomorrow I'm going to start cutting our production until things pick up. I can't afford bad sales *and* too much inventory."

"I'll help you deliver them," she said. "We can do it on our way to city hall."

I flipped the sign and locked the door. As I started boxing up our leftovers, I said, "I already spoke with Sherry Lance, but we can still talk to the mayor."

Grace looked hurt by the admission. "You went somewhere without me?"

"She came here," I said as I boxed the last donut. We had a six-dozen donut overage, one of the largest we'd had since I'd opened the donut shop. I hoped the church had room for them in their kitchen.

"How did that go? I have a hard time seeing Sherry in here."

"She didn't come in. You'd think I was selling something illegal from the way she reacted when I offered her a free donut."

"I know it's hard to believe, but donuts aren't to everyone's taste."

I studied her and said, "Sometimes it's like I don't even know you."

"Hey, not me, at least not anymore. You

151

know I love them. I'm talking about other people."

"I'll let you off the hook this time," I said, just as there was a pounding on the front door. Usually I try to keep from unlocking the door to customers once I've locked it, but I couldn't be picky at the moment.

When I saw who it was, I debated changing my mind.

Max, my ex, was standing there, waving a fifty-dollar bill in his hand.

"What does he want?" Grace asked, her dislike for Max evident in her voice.

"I'm not sure, but if it's donuts, I can't afford to turn him away."

"Well, I don't have to watch. I'll be in back with Emma."

"Okay, I'll call you when we're finished," I said.

I walked over to the door, but I didn't unlock it. "Is there something I can do for you, Max?"

"How many donuts do you have left?"

I glanced back at the boxes. "Six dozen." I grinned at him. "It's your lucky day. We're running a special after-hours sale. If you want one, you have to buy them all."

"That won't be a problem," he said. "Would this fifty cover it?"

"Absolutely," I said as I unlocked the

door. After I let him in, I asked, "Where did the money come from?"

"Buck Thister joined my theater group, and he wants to treat the cast to donuts. You wouldn't turn an old man down, would you?"

I hadn't met Buck yet, but I knew Max's theater group was full of retirees who loved to put on plays. My ex-husband generally fancied himself an actor, though most of the parts he got were for commercials, and when he wasn't working, he liked to direct. Fortunately, I'd been lucky enough, if you could call it that, to catch him with Darlene right after a big payday. Our divorce settlement had paid for the donut shop, so at least something good had come of it.

The fifty would be pure gravy, since I'd already discounted these particular donuts as a contribution, but honestly, I didn't think the church would mind, since they most likely were still eating the donuts I'd given them the day before. I unlocked the door, and took the fifty out of his hand.

As he started gathering up donut boxes, he asked, "Is this a good assortment?"

"It's a little heavy on glazed donuts and donut holes, but it's the best I can do on such short notice."

"It sounds great to me," he said. He

looked helplessly at me and asked, "Could you get the door for me?"

For that kind of money, I would have delivered them myself. As I held the door open, I asked, "What play are you doing this time?"

*"Teen Angel,"* he said with a grin. His troupe enjoyed going against expectations, and they did a really good job on every project they tackled. I'd especially enjoyed their version of *Romeo and Juliet,* and looked forward to seeing this production, as well. What I loved was their Sunday matinees, which allowed me to get off work in time for the show and still not miss my early bedtime. I had to take culture where I could get it, given my crazy work schedule.

"Thanks," he said. "You're a lifesaver."

"Glad I could help," I said as I relocked the door.

Grace popped her head out of the kitchen. "Is he gone?"

"Don't worry, it's safe now."

"What did he want?" she asked.

I noticed Emma was listening, as well. For once, her iPod earbuds were out while she was doing dishes.

"Donuts," I said simply.

"Is that *all* he wanted?"

"Grace, it doesn't matter, because that

was all he was going to get, and we both knew it. Now, if we're finished talking about this, grab a rag and start bussing tables. The sooner we get our work finished, the quicker we can get out of here."

Emma finished the last rack and drained the water. "Does that mean I can go, Suzanne?"

"Sure," I said. "What's going on? Do you have a big date this afternoon?"

"I wish," she answered wistfully. "I can't remember the last time I went out with someone."

Grace laughed. "I'm sure it's been weeks. What a tragedy. However do you stand it?"

She sighed heavily. "I know this drought can't last forever. And it's been eleven days, for your information. I'm willing to bet you've gone out more recently than that."

"Then you'd lose," Grace said, still smiling.

"You don't seem to be all that upset about it," Emma said, and then she must have realized how impertinent she sounded. "I'm sorry. Strike that. It's none of my business."

Grace smiled at her. "Don't worry about it. There's nobody here but us girls. To be honest with you, I'm kind of enjoying my break. It gives me a chance at a little perspective, you know?"

155

"I don't see how," Emma admitted.

"Me, either, but it sounds good, doesn't it?"

"If you two are finished commiserating," I said, "there's still work to do."

"I thought I could go," Emma protested.

"That was before you stuck around distracting us. One more chance, and then it's back to work."

"Bye," she said as she bolted for the door.

Grace and I were both laughing as I locked it behind her. I studied my friend for a few seconds, and then went against my own better judgment. I had a policy of not getting involved in her love life, but I couldn't help myself. "Would you like me to ask Jake if he's got any single friends?"

"Thanks for the offer, but I don't think so."

"What's wrong with Jake?"

She started wiping down tables as she said, "No offense, but I've seen what dating a police officer has done to you. If I ever have a boyfriend again, I want him around a little more than yours seems to manage."

"He's on vacation now," I said, finding it odd to have to defend Jake to her.

"Where did he go, Hawaii?"

"He's still in town," I admitted.

"And you worked today? Why don't you

shut the place down and have a little fun?"

"Thanks, but I've already had that particular lecture from my mother."

Grace nodded. "Enough said." As she finished the last table, she asked, "Are you ready to go to city hall?"

"What makes you think our fair mayor is there?"

"I was at the Boxcar having a late breakfast," Grace said, "and I heard his honor ordering lunch to be delivered at his desk. If we hurry, we might make it before he gets to his dessert."

"I'm game if you are," I said as I put the last plate away. The kitchen was in good shape, and the front was clean. There was just one more task I had to accomplish. "Once I get the register checked and the deposit made up, we're good to go."

"That's going to take forever," Grace said. "We can't wait that long."

"You haven't seen my receipts today," I said. "It's not going to take nearly as long as you might think."

I entered the sale to Max, counted my money, and ran the report off the cash register. Four minutes later, I had the deposit in my bag, and we were ready to go. It was lucky that things balanced out so perfectly, but I had to wonder if it might have had something to do with the fact that there hadn't been all that much to count.

I'd worry about that later. The only way I'd be able to fix it would be to get my customer base back, and I had a hunch that meant solving Lester Moorefield's murder. As I locked the door after we walked out onto the sidewalk, Grace asked, "Wasn't George supposed to meet us here, or did he already come by?"

"No, I haven't seen him all day. Let me give him a call."

"Let's at least get in my car first," Grace said. "I don't want anyone to overhear you."

"I've talked to George in public before," I said.

"Indulge me," she answered.

I did as she asked, and the second we got to her car, I dialed George's telephone number.

There was no answer, just four rings, and then it went to voice mail.

I waited for the beep, and said, "George, it's Suzanne. Grace and I are leaving Donut Hearts. Hopefully we'll catch up with you soon."

"That's odd," I said as I hung up.

"What's that?"

"George didn't answer his phone."

Grace shook her head. "He's a big boy,

Suzanne. George can take care of himself."

"I hope you're right."

As we drove to city hall, I couldn't help wondering what circumstances would keep George from touching base with us. Was he in trouble, or was he just involved in something at the moment that required his attention? Either way, I couldn't wait to speak with him again. I relied on George's advice and input, but most of all, I needed his heart. He'd believed in me in the past when everyone else had thought I was crazy, and I could use a little of that right now. I thought about calling Jake, but if he really was still asleep, I didn't want to be the one who woke him.

"Ladies, it's always a pleasure to see you." Cam Hamilton stood as we walked in, and the politician in him made him shake hands with both of us before we could sit down. Cam had been a high school football star once upon a time, but in the twenty years since, he'd added fifty pounds to his leanest playing weight. His hair hadn't changed, though, carefully cut and styled as always, and I doubted a trip through a wind tunnel would move a single hair out of place. Cam was a building contractor who specialized in small jobs. That left him plenty of time to pursue his passion of being our mayor, which was clear to anyone who knew him.

He frowned slightly as he said, "Funny, Polly didn't tell me I had visitors."

She hadn't been at her post, so we'd decided to barge on in and, hopefully, catch him off guard. "No one was out front," I said.

"That's fine," Cam said, though it was obvious it was anything but okay with him. "What can I do for you?" he asked once we were settled in.

"Lester Moorefield really went after you in an editorial not long ago, didn't he?"

Cam looked a little startled by the abruptness of Grace's question. I had planned on being a little smoother in bringing it up, but there was no going back now.

"We all know Lester was full of bluster," Cam said good-naturedly. "He loved stirring things up."

"What exactly did he say about you?" I asked. "I know it had something to do with where the new library is being built, but I was hoping you might be able to elaborate on what he said on the air."

Cam's smile faded, but only slightly. "Forgive me, but I'm curious why that concerns either one of you."

"Just think of us as a couple of civic-minded individuals," Grace said. How she kept a straight face, I'll never know.

Cam nodded. "The fact that folks around town are under the impression you had anything to do with his demise notwithstanding." He'd been looking directly at me as he'd said it.

"The question is still valid. There was a kernel of truth to everything Lester said in his editorials."

"So, you admit that you sell poison?"

"Any treat is harmful in excess," I said, weary of having to repeat that same argument over and over again. "It was some of the truth, just not all of it. What part of his editorial about you was true?"

Cam clearly didn't like me turning the tables on him. "Not a single word of it. I had nothing to do with the library placement. Look it up. It's a matter of public record."

"How did you feel about him after his attack on you?" I asked. "You must have been even madder than I was."

Cam tried to laugh it off. "Ladies, I get attacked all the time, and my motives are questioned as a matter of course. It's one of the prices we civil servants pay for serving our communities."

"Are you trying to tell us you didn't talk

to him after he lambasted you?" I asked. "Excuse me, but I find that hard to believe."

"We spoke," Cam reluctantly admitted. "What was said was between the two of us, though."

"I'm sure Chief Martin would be interested to hear it."

Cam sat up a little straighter in his chair. "Don't kid yourself. After all, the chief works for me."

"Funny, I thought we elected him."

"Of course," Cam quickly amended. "But he answers to me directly."

It was clear Grace wasn't going to let that go. "Do you believe that because of your position he's afraid to question you about the murder? Have you intimidated him that much?"

"Not at all," Cam said, clearly unhappy with the turn our talk had taken. He shuffled some papers on his desk, then said, "You'll have to forgive me, but I've got some rather pressing business I need to take care of. Was there anything else?"

"Just one thing," I said. "Where were you the night Lester was murdered?"

Cam grinned at me. "Good afternoon, ladies."

I was all for sitting there until he answered our question, but Grace stood, and I had no choice but to follow suit. Once we were outside, I asked, "Why did we just give up so quickly? I could have stayed there all day if it meant getting an answer to our question."

"That's the problem, though. He wasn't about to tell us. If the mayor's going to give anyone his alibi, it's going to have to be our police chief."

"That doesn't exactly comfort me," I said. "Even if he gets one, the chief's not about to share it with us."

"We've given the mayor something to think about," Grace said. "What more could we do?"

"I suppose you're right," I said reluctantly, "but I don't have to like it. There's something about that man I've never fully trusted."

"Could it be that he's a politician?"

"Maybe," I replied. "He was lying; I'm sure of it."

"Probably, since his lips were moving," Grace said. "We need more information before we tackle him again."

"Any idea where we might find some?" I asked.

"You're the brains behind this group. I'm just a foot soldier."

"More like an actress and an instigator," I said.

"I've been called worse, believe me." She hesitated when we got back to her car. "I mean it, Suzanne. You're so much better at figuring things out than I'll ever be. Where do you think we should go next?"

"The number of people who wanted Lester to come to harm is staggering, isn't it? So far, we've got three people he went after on the radio, we've got his estranged wife, we've got former investors he robbed, and others still. I wonder why he was on the outs with that builder?"

"We could always find out," Grace said. "Who knows the man?"

"We'll have to ask Cara," I said. "She produced all of Lester's broadcasts."

As we drove toward the radio station, my telephone rang. I'd had it set to laughter at one point, and then to a song I loved, but I'd grown tired of both of them, so for the moment, it was a simple ring, the same sound I'd loved growing up. That was before the telephone brought bad news into my life; as a child, I'd always wondered who was calling our home, and what news they were bringing.

"Hello," I said.

"Hey, Suzanne."

"Jake," I answered, "I wondered if I was ever going to hear from you today. Boy, when you go on vacation, you really go all out, don't you? Did you just get up?"

His voice wasn't happy when he replied. "I wish. No, I've been up since eight. I got a call from my boss. He canceled my vacation. It turns out I've got a case."

"That's terrible," I said. "I was looking forward to spending a little time with you." It had taken me some time to come to terms with my boyfriend's demanding schedule, but it wasn't all that easy getting someone to put up with my odd hours, so I really couldn't complain. "Where are you going, and how long will you be gone?"

"That's the thing. I'm not going anywhere. I've been assigned to Lester Moorefield's murder investigation."

# CHAPTER 9

"What?" I asked incredulously. "Jake, I'm in this thing up to my eyebrows."

"I know that," he said. At least he was upset by it, too. "My boss was very specific. I've been ordered to give Chief Martin any assistance I can."

"You've got a conflict, though," I said. "Doesn't your boss realize that?"

There was dead silence on the other end of the line, and something suddenly occurred to me. "He does know we're dating, doesn't he?"

"Suzanne, my supervisor could care less about my love life. Even if I told him about you, I doubt it would change anything."

"You have to try, Jake." Working on a case had brought us together, but it had also nearly torn us apart in the past. But maybe I wasn't looking at this the right way. Jake was good at what he did, and I wasn't above getting another helping hand. After all, I had no trouble with Grace and George pitching in. "You don't have any choice. I can see that. Is there any way we can work together on the case?"

"You have to be reasonable, Suzanne," he said, a request I'd never enjoyed hearing from anyone, let alone my boyfriend. "I'm working in my official capacity as an investigating officer. I can't just feed you whatever I uncover."

"I can see that," I said, "but there's got to be some way we can work together, at least a little."

There was a pause, and then he said, "I might be able to tell you if you're working on a dead end, but I'm not sure what else I can do."

"If that's the best you can do, I'll take it." We were nearing the radio station parking lot. "Listen, I've got to go."

"I'm not trying to be stubborn about this," he said.

"I know," I answered, and then hung up.

"So, I take it your boyfriend is on the case, too," Grace said as I hung up the telephone.

"We can't let that stop us. Jake is good at what he does, but so are we. I still think we can help solve this case."

"And how do you think he's going to feel about that?"

"I'm not sure. Why don't we ask him? He's sitting in the radio station parking lot," I answered as I pointed to my boyfriend, leaning against the side of his car.

We parked, and then approached him.

"Have any tidbits to share so far?" I asked him with a big grin.

"It's a little too early for that."

I nodded, and then gestured to the radio station. "Is Cara inside?"

"Why do you ask?"

"We're old friends," I said.

With a wry smile, he said, "You're going to keep digging into this, even with me on the case." When I didn't say anything, he asked, "Aren't you going to answer me?"

"I didn't hear a question anywhere in there," I replied, returning his smile. I glanced over at Grace, who pretended to be on a telephone call. I knew better. There was no way she was going to miss this exchange.

Jake took a deep breath, and then asked, "Suzanne, are you going to keep investigating this case, even though I've been assigned to it?"

"I'm just asking my friends some questions," I said. "Surely there's nothing wrong with that."

"Just try to stay out of trouble, okay?"

168

"Hey, I'm not making any promises," I said.

After he left, Grace's telephone call magically ended. "What was that all about?" she asked me.

"Don't try to act innocent with me. You were eavesdropping."

"Of course I was," she answered with a smile. "But I didn't catch that last part, and that's the best part of the scene. How did it end?"

"Well, he didn't lock us up," I said as I started toward the station door.

"He's not all that happy with you investigating, is he?"

I shrugged. "He probably has a point, but I can't worry about that right now."

Grace put a hand on my arm, and I stopped. She looked me in the eye and said, "Suzanne, this isn't worth ruining your life over. Jake is capable, we both know that. Maybe we should step back and let him handle things."

I shook my head. "That's not going to work. I know Jake is good at what he does, but he doesn't know these people like we do. There's not much chance they're going to open up with him like they could with us. We can get to the bottom of this ourselves."

"If you're sure."

"I don't think we have much choice, do you?"

As I buzzed the door for admission, a part of me wondered if Grace was right. Was I taking a chance of sabotaging my relationship with my investigation? Was I really just going after Lester's killer, or was a part of me pushing Jake away? No, that was ridiculous. I was growing attached to the man; there was no way I wanted to get rid of him. But I meant what I'd said. I wasn't going to try to do anything stupid like try to catch the killer myself without any backup, but if I could find out something that might help Jake and the police chief catch a murderer, I couldn't stand by and do nothing. My business had already dropped off enough for me to feel it, and if Max hadn't come along with someone else's money earlier, I wouldn't have made my basic expenses today. I had to do something.

I just hoped that Jake realized that.

His blessing was clearly too much to ask for.

"Cara, it's Suzanne," I said as she finally answered the buzzer.

There was a long hesitation before she answered. "I'm sorry, but I'm tied up right

170

now. I can't really talk."

"This will just take a second," I said.

"Perhaps you could call for an appointment," she said after another moment's delay. "You have my number here, right?"

Cara definitely sounded out of sorts. What was going on with her? "I do."

"Then I suggest you phone ahead next time."

Before I could reply, the intercom died.

Grace looked at me quizzically. "What was that all about?"

"I'm not sure, but I'm going to find out." I punched in the directory on my phone and found her number. I'd used it in the past when dealing with Lester.

When she answered, I asked, "Cara? Is everything okay?"

"I'm sorry, but she's out right now," Cara said. "I expect her sometime after three, if you'd like to try again then. She's purchasing a grill. You can speak with her then."

"You'd like to meet me at three at the Boxcar Grill, is that what you're saying?"

"Yes, that's correct. Good-bye."

Grace hadn't been able to hear Cara's replies. "What's going on?"

I looked at my watch. "She'll meet us at the Boxcar in an hour," I said. "It's all very cryptic, isn't it?"

"What should we do in the meantime?" Grace asked.

"A hamburger might be nice," I said as my stomach rumbled a little.

"Food would be good," she agreed, so we drove to the Boxcar to eat, and then wait for Cara. If we timed things right, we'd easily be finished by the time she arrived and we could pursue more leads.

Trish met us at the door with a grin. "Good afternoon. It's a little late in the day for lunch for you, isn't it, Suzanne?"

"Better late than never," I said.

"Especially if you're coming here." She waved a pair of menus in the air. "Is there any need for me to even bring these?"

Grace smiled at her. "We can do better than that. You don't even need to walk us to a table. We'll order here and save you the trip."

"That's what I like, powerful women who know what they want. Let me guess. Two cheeseburgers, fries, and a pair of Cokes."

I started to nod, and then said, "Let's shake things up a little. Bring me a sweet tea instead."

"Make it two," Grace said.

Trish shook her head. "Sometimes it's like I don't even know you two anymore. Two teas coming right up."

We found a table away from the other diners and settled in. I loved the Boxcar Grill, and not just for its convenience and its cuisine. There was something about the old railcar that fit in nicely with my converted train depot, and I felt it was a kindred spirit to Donut Hearts.

Just after we'd sat down, Emily Hargraves, the pretty brunette who ran Two Cows and a Moose Newsstand, came in.

"Hey Emily," I called out. "Want to join us?"

"If you're sure you don't mind," Emily said. "I already ordered. Sometimes I don't mind eating alone, but I almost didn't come in here today. It can get old, can't it?"

"That's why Grace and I are together so much," I said. "It's never lonely with two."

Grace jumped into the conversation. "How are the guys doing?" The guys she was referring to were three stuffed animals Emily had had since she was a child, and which had provided the name for her newsstand.

"They're doing great. In fact, it's about time to come up with some new outfits for them."

I laughed. "I can't tell you how much I look forward to seeing them dressed up. Halloween was great."

"I liked the Santa outfits at Christmas," Grace said.

"They're in little green suits at the moment, but I'm ready for a change."

I took a sip of my iced tea, and then asked, "You dressed them up as Martians?"

"Are you kidding? They never would have tolerated that. Well, not Moose. Cow and Spots are 'go with the flow' kind of guys. No, I made them St. Patrick's Day outfits, along with green top hats sporting shamrocks."

"What's next?"

She thought about it a moment, and then admitted, "I have no earthly idea. It's too soon for their July Fourth outfits. They're all going to be Uncle Sams this year."

"I can't wait to see it," I said.

After Trish brought Emily a Coke and left, she said, "Suzanne, I know you think I'm crazy naming my place after my stuffed animals."

"That's not true," I said. "I was just a little worried at first that it might confuse folks about what kind of shop you owned."

"Maybe at first," Emily said, "but now I get a lot of people coming in just to see what the three of them are up to, and while they are there, they pick up a few things along the way. You'd be amazed by how my sales jump whenever the three of them put on something new."

"That's brilliant," I said. "I'm starting to wish that I'd thought of that."

Emily smiled. "Sorry, but it's taken."

Trish brought three plates of food, and as she distributed them, Emily said, "That was fast."

"We aim to please," Trish said.

After the three of us finished eating, Emily asked, "Can I walk out with you?"

"That sounds great, but we've got to hang around for a meeting."

She nodded as she stood. "Thanks for letting me join you. It was great fun."

"You are welcome to join us anytime," I said.

Trish bussed our table, and then asked, "Can I get you to-go cups for that tea?"

"Do you mind if we linger a little longer?" I asked.

She looked around the nearly empty restaurant. "You can stay until four, for all I care. I'll be back in a second to top off your glasses."

We didn't have long to wait. Less than five minutes later, Cara walked in. She found us in an instant and hurried to join us.

"I'm sorry about all of the intrigue," she said, "but I couldn't let you in."

"What's going on?" I asked. "I like playing spy as much as the next gal, but I like to know about it ahead of time."

"The station manager is on the warpath. He thinks there's been entirely too much public access in our work area, and he's really cracking down."

"At least you won't have to put up with it for very long," Grace said.

"I've got some good news on that front. I got a new job," Cara said. "Gail the Gardening Lady fired her producer the second she heard I was free and hired me on the spot."

"That's great," I said. At least it was for everyone but Gail's old producer.

Cara must have seen something in my gaze. "Don't worry about Jimmy. He came in drunk more times than he was sober. He said he needed it to get through Granny Gail's show every day."

I had to suppress a smile. I didn't approve of the way he handled his situation, but I could see why he'd started drinking. There was a quality to Gail's voice that was like a fingernail running down a blackboard to me, and how she'd ever found a career in radio was beyond me. "Well, at least you're employed."

Cara sighed. "It's not perfect, but it will do, at least for now. What did you want to see me about? I've already told you everything I know."

"We were wondering about the name of the builder Lester went after recently," Grace said.

"Is there any chance you've got his contact information?" I asked.

Cara nodded. "It's Vern Yancey. He lives in Hudson Creek, and he should be in the book."

"You don't sound too pleased about him," I said.

"Usually I thought Lester was stretching it when he went after someone, but I met Vern once. The man deserved the lashing he got, as far as I'm concerned. Be careful if you go talk to him. I think he's got some criminal ties that could be bad for you. He doesn't say much, but things seem to happen when he's around."

"Thanks, we'll watch our step."

Cara glanced at her watch. "My break is almost over. I have to get back to the station."

"Can we order you something to go?" I asked.

"I've already eaten, but thanks for the offer. I'll take a rain check, though," she called out as she left the grill.

Grace and I paid our tabs as we left, turning down more tea for the road. If I kept drinking, I wouldn't be able to sit still for the rest of the day.

"I haven't been to Hudson Creek in years," I said as we drove to the small town thirty minutes south of April Springs.

"You're in for a treat, then. They've been having some kind of revival there. There are all kinds of antiques shops now, and from what I hear, they're even starting to get some tourists in."

"Why didn't I hear about this? I love antiquing."

"Suzanne, in order to have any semblance of a life, you have to actually leave that donut shop of yours from time to time to see what's out there."

"True," I said. "How did you find out about it?"

"A friend of mine lives there," she said, and didn't add anything to her explanation.

I knew what that meant without having to ask. "What's his name?"

She glanced over at me. "What are you talking about? What makes you think it's a man? I have women friends, too."

"Okay, then, what's her name?"

Grace smiled slightly. "It's Bill."

"Imagine that, a girl named Bill," I said with an open grin.

"My point was that it wasn't necessarily a man."

"I got it," I said. "Why didn't I ever hear about this guy?"

She tapped the steering wheel center with her thumbs. "We just went out a few times, and there was nothing really to report. He's a nice enough fellow, but it turned out we didn't have that much in common."

"Maybe he can give us a little background on Vern. Hudson Creek isn't that big a place. It's probably smaller than April Springs."

"We could ask," she said.

"But you'd rather we didn't."

"No, it's fine. We both agreed it wasn't going anywhere, so there were no hard feelings when we stopped dating."

"So then where do we find him?"

Grace made a turn, and then said, "He runs a shop on Elm. It's part of Antiques Row, and it's called Yesterday's Treasures."

When we got within the city limits, I could see that Grace was right. Gone were the empty buildings and the shabby storefronts I'd remembered. In their place, antiques shops lined both sides of the road, with the occasional odd store thrown into the mix, including a café and a small bookstore. "It looks kind of charming," I said.

As Grace parked in front of her friend's shop, she said, "It surely is a vast improvement over what they had before. Let's go see what Bill has to say."

The antiques shop was well lit and uncluttered, something I wasn't used to seeing in that kind of store. It was clear that Bill liked things neat. There were carefully laid out sections marked Tools, Books, Furniture, Collectibles, and several other categories. A tall and willowy man came out of the back office as we walked in, his blue eyes lighting up when he recognized Grace.

"As I live and breathe," he said as he took Grace's hands in his own. "I haven't seen you in forever. How are you?"

"I'm well. And you?"

He pointed around his shop. "Contrary to how it looks at the moment, business is booming." He turned his gaze toward me. "Who's your friend?"

"This is Suzanne Hart," she said, and Bill looked delighted.

"You own Donut Hearts," he said with a smile.

"You know it?" I asked. For the life of me, I didn't recognize him. Not that I knew every customer who came through my door, but I expected him to at least look familiar. "Have we met?"

"No, but I have a friend who buys donuts from you just about every week, and sometimes she's good enough to share with me."

"Who is it?"

"Lisa Grambling."

"I know Lisa well," I said. She was a short, curvy woman with a ready smile and a constant yen for my donuts.

He patted his lean stomach. "Sometimes I wish she wasn't such a big fan of yours. Are you two ladies looking for something in particular, or are you just browsing?"

"We're looking for some information," Grace said.

Bill looked around, pretending to study his shop. "Let's see, I'm not sure I carry that. The closest I come to that is my book section, but I've got a hunch that's not what you're after."

"It's about Vern Yancey," I said.

That's when Bill's expression tightened, the smile dropping off his face as though it had never been there.

"Do you know him?" I asked.

"I'm sorry, but I can't help you."

We weren't about to let it go at that, though. Evidently we'd done the right thing coming to Bill first.

"It's okay," Grace said. "I promise, this is just among friends."

It was clear he realized that we weren't going anywhere without a fight.

Apparently he didn't mind having one.

"I'm sorry, but I'm going to have to ask you to leave," he said.

# CHAPTER 10

Grace said softly, "I know we didn't date a long time, but surely you know me well enough to realize that you can trust me, Bill. I wouldn't ask if it wasn't important."

"I said I don't have anything to say to you," he declared.

I looked around the shop. "There's no one here but the three of us. Anything you tell us will be kept quiet. You have our word."

Bill frowned, scratched his cheek, and then said, "I'm not a bad guy. I'd like to help you, but I can't risk it."

"We understand," I said as I tugged at Grace's arm.

Instead of leaving as I'd suggested, Grace turned to him. "Bill, it's safe to tell us. I promise neither one of us will say a word to anyone. Wouldn't it be nice not to be afraid, just once?"

Bill lowered his voice, though no one would have been able to hear him had he decided to shout out his reply. "Yeah, maybe it would. I don't own this building. I lease it, along with just about everyone else on the strip. Take three guesses who owns everything you see."

"I just need one," I said. "So what if Vern is your landlord? He can't throw you out for talking about him."

Bill shook his head. "You have no idea who you're dealing with. Two months ago Connie Branton made a crack about him at the Popover Diner, and the next day she got an eviction notice. It seemed that she wasn't in compliance with a clause none of us even recognized. Her aisles were an inch and half too narrow, and she had seven days to vacate the premises. I knew I should have gotten a lawyer to check out the contract I signed with him, but it was such a good deal, I couldn't afford to say no. It's the same situation the rest of us are in. Vern's taken over most of this street, and there's not a thing any of us can do about it. Now do me a favor and forget I said a word to you."

"We can do that," I said as I started for the door.

Grace touched his arm lightly. "I'm really sorry. I shouldn't have pushed you like that."

Bill forced out a smile. "It's not that bad.

As long as we don't make waves, things are good here."

We were at the door when I stopped and turned around. "Any idea where Vern might be right now?"

Bill's face paled slightly. "You're not going to talk to him, are you?"

"That's why we're here," I said.

"Don't mention my name. Promise me that."

"He won't hear it from us," Grace said. "Does he have an office around here?"

"He does, but he won't be there. Vern is building a new home on Lakeside Road, and he's been spending all of his time out there on the site." Bill reluctantly gave us directions, and then said, "But you'd both be doing me a favor if you just forget about him altogether."

"I wish we could," I said, "but like I told you before, it's important."

After we were in the car following Bill's directions, Grace said, "I can't believe how spooked Bill was. If you had asked me before we went in, I would have said nothing could rattle him."

"It sounds as though he has a right to be jumpy," I said. "No wonder Lester went after Vern. It explains Cara's reaction to him, too."

"He sounds like a real charmer."

"I know it's not going to be particularly pleasant, Grace, but we have to get a feel for what the man's capable of."

She shook her head. "I think we already know that, don't you?"

"Being a bully doesn't make him a murderer."

She frowned a second, and then said, "It doesn't clear him, either."

We got to the house under construction, and it was even larger than Bill had told us. It was hard to believe that anyone in Hudson Creek could afford that kind of place, but if Vern Yancey owned as much of the town as Bill said, it was entirely possible.

We got out of the car as a brand-new black Ford pickup came down the drive. The man behind the wheel stopped when he saw us, and rolled his window down.

"Help you?" he asked.

"We're looking for Vern Yancey," I said.

"Found him," he answered. Vern was clearly a man of few words. I couldn't see a great deal of him, but what I saw wasn't the least bit intimidating. He was in his fifties, a small and wiry man with wisps of hair hanging doggedly onto his scalp.

"Do you have a second?" Grace asked.

"About that," he answered. It was clear

that he had no interest in getting out of the car, so we were going to have to interview him right there.

"It's about Lester Moorefield," I said.

Vern spat in the dirt. "Got what he deserved, if you ask me."

This wasn't going to be easy. "He came after you, too, didn't he?"

That sparked a little interest in his gaze. "You?"

"I own a donut shop, and he called my donuts poison."

Vern nodded, whether in simple acknowledgment or sympathy, I couldn't say.

"We were wondering if the police have asked you for an alibi yet," Grace said.

"Nope."

"Do you have one?" I asked.

He stared holes through me, rolled up his window, and drove off.

I looked at Grace. "That went well, didn't it?"

"Probably what we should have expected," I answered. "I'm going to tell Jake about him. I'm curious to see how tough Vern is when he's talking to a state police investigator."

"He can't say much less, can he? What should we do next?"

I checked my watch. "I think we need to

head back to April Springs. There's nothing else we can learn here."

"I'm fine with that," Grace said. "It's just really frustrating when people won't talk to us."

"They're not under any obligation to," I said. "We just have to take the crumbs we can get, and do our best with that. I'm trying to discover things Jake might miss, not solve the case. If I can give him a tip or two and not have to talk to a murderer, I'm fine with that."

"Okay, then. Home it is. When are you going to talk to Jake?"

"I'm not sure," I said as we drove back home. "I'll have to find the right moment."

Grace laughed. "Good luck with that."

As we drove back into town, I reflected that I was happy I lived in April Springs and not Hudson Creek. Our community, though small, was diverse enough that no one person could exert that much influence over us. Then again, I wondered how many people in Hudson Creek were actually aware of what Vern Yancey was doing. Could there be an equally strong power at work behind the scenes in our town? If there was, I didn't know about it, and frankly, I liked it that way. There were times when ignorance was bliss, and I was willing to count this as one of them. I had enough to worry about in my own circle without taking on any more concerns. As long as I had my mother, my friends, and my donuts, I could be happy with the way the rest of the world operated.

"Suzanne, I think we found George," Grace said as she neared Donut Hearts. His sedan was parked in the spot beside mine.

"I wonder how long he's been waiting," I said. As we got closer, I saw that George was slumped over in his seat.

Had something happened to him while we'd been off chasing clues? If he was dead, particularly because he'd been helping me, I'd never be able to forgive myself.

I held my breath as I tapped on the car window. "George? Are you all right?"

To my great relief, he jerked up in his seat. "Sorry about that," he said as he got out. "I must have dozed off."

"I'm the one who's been up since one-thirty," I said. "If anybody deserves a nap, it's me."

"I've been having a little trouble sleeping lately," he admitted. "Enough about that. Where have you two been?"

"We just got back from Hudson Creek," Grace said.

189

"I never did like that town."

"It's an interesting place," I said. "We were interviewing a suspect there. Have you ever heard of Vern Yancey?"

"Why do you think I don't care for Hudson Creek? He's a cocky little bantam rooster of a man. I arrested him once for speeding, and he threatened me with just about everything short of public hanging if I didn't tear up the ticket."

"Did it stick?" Grace asked.

"You bet, but he's been gunning for me ever since. I'm sorry I didn't get in on that interview with you. I would have loved to put the screws to him again."

"You may get your chance later," I said. "Did you have any luck with the investors Lester scammed?"

George shook his head. "All but one is dead. This happened a long time ago, and he targeted senior citizens. The guy who's still alive is a pistol, though. He's living in Asheville, and he's not afraid who knows he threatened Lester. I think he was kind of proud of it, if you ask me."

"Is he a viable suspect?" I asked.

George shook his head. "The man's in a wheelchair staying in an assisted living home, so he doesn't have access to transportation. The night Lester was murdered, he was in the hospital for observation. From what I was able to find out, we can strike that entire line of inquiry off our list."

"How about the other side of the coin? Any idea who might have targeted him as a victim?"

George shook his head. "As far as I could tell, everyone involved in the case believed that he spent that money a long time ago. There wasn't anything to steal."

I nodded. "You were productive, then."

"I'm not so sure about that," George said as he stretched his neck a little. Evidently his nap had put a crick in his shoulders.

"We can eliminate two entire types of suspects," I said. "That's pretty good in my book. Now we can focus on some of the folks who had the opportunity and the motivation to strangle him."

"It's still a pretty long list," George said, "but I'll keep digging."

"Touch base tomorrow," I said, and he nodded as he got into his car and drove off.

Once he was gone, Grace asked, "Was it my imagination, or was George a little touchy just then?"

"We caught him napping," I said. "That had to be a little embarrassing."

"I suppose so. Any plans tonight?"

"Are you asking ever so subtly if I'm seeing Jake?"

"That, among other things," she said.

"Grace, I wish I knew. Jake gets kind of odd when he's on a case, especially when it involves me."

"And you're a little odd all of the time," she said with an affectionate smile.

"Coming from you, I'll take that as a compliment."

"I don't know why you wouldn't, that's how I meant it."

I glanced at her and asked, "How about you? I'm sure you have to have something going on."

"You bet I do. I'm taking a long hot bath, ordering in, and not doing anything the rest of the evening. It sounds like a little slice of paradise to me."

"I'll see you tomorrow, then."

"Tomorrow," she said, and drove off.

I got into my Jeep and headed home. I hoped Momma had cooked something special tonight. I was in the mood for one of her feasts, and if I was lucky, that was exactly what I was going to get.

I was already dreaming about what delicious meal I was about to eat when I slammed on the brakes of the Jeep.

A police cruiser was parked in our driveway, and I raced up the steps, dreading the thought that something had happened to my mother.

"Is everything all right?" I asked breathlessly as I burst into our living room.

Momma was sitting on the couch, and Chief Martin was in my favorite chair. Momma looked surprised. "Of course it is. Why shouldn't it be, Suzanne?"

After my heart stopped racing, I said, "I came home and found a police car in my driveway. Forgive me if I panicked."

The police chief said, "This isn't a professional call."

"Phillip was just leaving," my mother said.

It was clear that was news to the chief, but he took the hint and stood, retrieving his hat. "We'll talk more later," he said to my mother.

"Perhaps," she said.

One eyebrow shot up, but then he nodded, and headed for the door. "Good-bye, Suzanne."

"Bye," I said.

After he was gone, I asked, "What was that about?"

"What are you talking about?"

"You're kidding, right? I didn't mean to interrupt anything. Next time leave a dishtowel hanging on the front door, would you?

You nearly gave me a heart attack."

It was amusing to watch her face redden. "It wasn't like that."

"Not at the moment, but who knows what might have happened if I'd just given you a little more time? Come on, I told you it was okay with me."

"And I said I wasn't entirely certain that I was fine with it," she said, using that tone of voice that normally meant I should drop it.

I wasn't about to, but then I saw her expression, and decided that it wasn't fair to pick on her for doing exactly what I'd recommended. "Any ideas for dinner? I could take us out if you'd like."

"I thought I might reheat some chili. It won't be long before it's too hot for it. What do you say?"

"I say yum," I answered. "Let's eat out on the front porch." Sometimes when the weather was nice, Momma and I ate outside where we could take in the beauty of the park while we dined.

"That's an excellent idea," she said. "You set the places, and I'll get it ready. We'll be eating in fifteen minutes."

We beat that by two minutes, and as we sat down to our meal, I looked out at the park and said, "Your grandfather was a pretty smart fellow building this house next to the park."

"There wasn't a park here when he built it," Momma said as she added a little sour cream to her bowl. I was a purist, but Momma even added pasta to her chili bowl sometimes. She'd urged me to try it, but so far I'd managed to resist her suggestion.

"That makes sense. Otherwise they probably wouldn't have let him build it this close." My mother smiled, so I asked, "What is it?"

"I can't believe I never told you this story. You've got things reversed. He used to own all of this, all the way to the tracks."

I thought about all the land that encompassed. "And he sold it? Why? Did he need the money?"

"On the contrary, this was a small fraction of his holdings. He had foresight, that's all. After he bought the land, he built our cottage, and then deeded the park to the city."

"Sounds like he was a real humanitarian," I said.

"Not particularly. He loved trees and grass and flowers, but he hated their upkeep. By putting the park here, he got the benefits of a beautiful piece of property without having to lift a finger maintaining it."

"Didn't he mind the people being here all

of the time?"

"From what I understand," my mother said, "that was part of the enjoyment for him. Long after everyone else went home, he had the best front yard in seven counties. Cyrus was a crafty old fellow."

"Did you get to spend much time with him growing up?" I asked. He'd been dead long before I came along.

"I was ten when he died," she said. "Still, we spent a great deal of time here together. He sold off most of his land, but this place was always special to him. My family moved in here a month after he was gone, and I swear I could still smell those wintergreen mints he loved all over the place."

I looked carefully at my mother. "Are you saying you believe in ghosts?"

She laughed. "Even if I did, my grandfather wouldn't be one of them. He was always ready for the next challenge, and didn't dwell on the past. He nearly lost everything at one point in his life, but my father told me that he never gave it a second thought. He just rolled up his sleeves and got back to work."

"He sounds like a cool guy," I said.

"He was that."

After we were finished eating, I stood and began gathering bowls and glasses. Momma put a hand on my arm. "Those can wait," she said. "I need to talk to you."

"Those words are never followed with good news, are they?" I asked as I sat back down.

"This isn't good or bad; it just is. Phillip has asked me to have dinner with him tomorrow night."

"Is the divorce final?" I asked.

"As of today," Momma said. "That's why he came by."

I whistled. "Boy, you have to give him credit. He didn't waste much time asking you out, did he?"

"I thought you approved."

"Of him, or of you dating? Both, if that's what you want. What did you say?"

"I was about to answer when you rushed through the door like you were on fire."

I suddenly felt bad about that. "I'm so sorry."

Momma smiled at me. "Are you kidding me? You saved me from answering. I could have kissed you when you walked in."

"What was your answer going to be?"

She shrugged. "I honestly hadn't made up my mind one way or the other, and now I don't have to."

"I saw the look in his eye. He's not going to give up that easily."

"But for tonight he will," she said.

"Shh," I said to her.

"Suzanne, are you shushing me?"

I pointed to the park. There, on the edge of the forest that abutted it, stood a fawn, its golden coat shimmering in the dusk.

We watched the young deer for what felt like an hour but was most likely only a few minutes before it caught our scent and bolted back into the woods.

"Thank you, Great-grandfather," I said softly.

"I couldn't agree more," Momma said.

The conversation was over, the spell of it broken by the deer's disappearance. We gathered the dirty dishes up and headed inside. I was glad we'd had that talk. We didn't do enough of that these days, and I hoped the presence of a new man in her life — whoever he might be — wouldn't interfere with the time we spent together. One of the real pleasures of moving back home was getting reacquainted with my mother. I'd left her, filled with optimism about my new life with Max, and I'd returned more than a little worse for the wear. Coming back with those battle scars had presented a silver lining, though. For the most part, my mother had accepted me more as an equal than as a child, and I delighted in getting to know her as an adult. Sure, sometimes we slipped back in our well-worn roles of mother and daughter, but usually just in times of great stress.

Unfortunately, lately great stress was just about all that I was feeling.

I thought about pursuing more leads before I went to bed, but I was so worn out that I wasn't at all certain I was thinking clearly. What I needed was a good night's sleep.

Unfortunately, that wasn't in the cards for me.

# DROP DONUTS

This is a good basic drop donut. Unlike the baked or yeast donuts, these are hard to make into a traditional donut shape without a dropper, and even then the results can vary. Most days I make these, I use the standard two-spoon technique described below. Some folks like icing or glaze on theirs, but I just sprinkle a little powdered sugar and enjoy!

## Ingredients

1 1/2 cups all purpose flour
1/2 cup sugar (white)
1 egg, beaten
1/2 teaspoon baking powder
1/2 teaspoon baking soda
1/4 teaspoon nutmeg
Dash of salt
1 teaspoon vanilla
1 cup buttermilk (2% or whole milk will also do)
1/2 cup milk (2% or whole milk will also do)

## Directions

Heat canola oil to 360 degrees while you mix the batter. Sift the dry ingredients (flour, salt, baking powder, baking soda, and nutmeg) together, then stir in the buttermilk, milk, sugar, vanilla, and the beaten egg. When the ingredients are incorporated, take a teaspoon of batter and rake it into the fryer with another spoon. If the dough doesn't rise soon, gently nudge it with a chopstick, being careful not to splatter oil. After two minutes, check, and then flip, frying for another minute on the other side. These times may vary given too many factors to count, so keep a close eye on the donuts.

Makes about a dozen small donuts.

# CHAPTER 11

"Hello?" I managed to ask after grabbing for and completely missing the phone by my bed. "Hello?" I repeated. I'd been asleep about an hour, just long enough to get into a relaxed state of being, and one of the worst times to wake up.

"I can't believe I just did that. Suzanne, I forgot the time completely," Jake said apologetically.

"Don't worry about it," I said as I sat up in my bed. "It's great to hear from you anytime. I was hoping you'd call." I knew I was on the phone and he couldn't see me, but I still ran my fingers through my hair in an effort to tame it. "I'd love to talk to you. How was your day?"

"Not nearly as pleasant as I'd hoped," he admitted. "I wanted to spend some time with you, but instead I was with your chief of police all day."

"You couldn't have been with him all

day," I said.

"What do you mean?"

"He was here when I got home," I explained. "From what I could gather, he was asking Momma out on a date."

"His divorce was final today, and he's trying to make a move on her tonight? Wow, that's really fast, isn't it?"

"I suppose if you look at it in one way it is, but when you consider the fact that he's been in love with her since grade school, I'm guessing he decided he's finally waited long enough."

"Does that mean you approve?" I could hear the hint of a smile in Jake's words, and I loved the sound.

"I don't exactly disapprove," I said.

"We both know that's not the same thing."

"We do at that. I missed seeing you today."

"I missed you, too."

After a slight pause, he asked, "You were pretty busy yourself, weren't you?"

"I ran a few errands after work. Why?"

"I ran into Vern Yancey twenty minutes after you did. He wasn't pleased with you and Grace grilling him."

"That's surprising."

"What, that he didn't like answering your questions?"

"No," I said, "that he even acknowledged

that we'd spoken. He's not exactly the most forthright man in the world, is he?"

"He does enjoy his monosyllabic responses."

"Wow, that's a big word for a cop to be using," I said, hoping he could hear my smile, as well.

"I got a dictionary for Christmas by mistake, so I thought I might as well put it to good use."

"Well done," I said. "Did Vern tell you anything special, like providing an alibi for the night of the murder?"

"He gave me something, but it's going to be tough to check out."

"What is it? Maybe I can help."

Jake laughed. "Nice try, but I think I can manage it on my own."

"If you want any more suspects to look at, I've got a nice list I'm building."

"I'm sure you do."

I suddenly ached to see him. It was hard enough when he was out of town, but having him in April Springs just made me want to see him more. "If you want to come over, I could be ready in five minutes."

"Not this late."

"It's barely past nine," I said.

"Which is close to midnight your time, and neither one of us wants to see the carriage turn into a pumpkin. Go to sleep. We'll get together sometime tomorrow, even if it's just over a cup of coffee and a donut. My treat."

I laughed at that. "Wow, you really know how to turn a girl's head."

"What can I say, I'm quite the catch."

"Now if you can just get someone to chase you," I said, giggling for a moment like a schoolgirl.

"If you promise to try, I won't run very fast."

"You'd better not. Good night, Jake."

"Good night, Suzanne."

Before he could hang up, I said, "Thanks for calling."

"In spite of the hour?"

"Because of it. It's really nice hearing your voice just before I go to sleep."

After I hung up, I pulled the covers a little tighter around me. There was something nagging at me in the back of my mind, and just as I drifted off to sleep, I realized what it was. Jake hadn't warned me off the case, something that he'd said every time I'd snooped into someone's murder in the past. Either he was slipping, or my boyfriend was starting to understand me a little better. All of the warnings and threats he could muster wouldn't stop me from digging into Lester's murder, and it appeared that he was finally realizing that.

Somehow, it made drifting off to sleep even sweeter.

"I love this time of night," Emma Blake said as we took our break the next morning, standing outside the donut shop in the dark at a quarter till four. "It's so peaceful."

"Technically, it's morning," I said, "but I have to agree. The town seems so quiet and content, doesn't it?"

"As long as Happy Crane hasn't started delivering his newspapers yet. I don't know why Dad puts up with him. The man hasn't had a new car in twenty years, and that clunker he's driving now backfires every twenty feet."

"I don't know; I think it's reassuring to hear him come by." Emma's father's newspaper seemed to exist as a way to distribute ads to its subscribers, but Ray Blake was always on the lookout for news. If he could ever manage to scoop the papers in Hickory and Charlotte on a hot story, he claimed that he would give his newspapers away free that day, but so far he hadn't given out a single one. "Is Ray trying to solve Lester's murder?"

"I'm sure he wouldn't mind if he could

break the story, but Dad doesn't like to get directly involved with murder investigations."

"Then he's smarter than I am," I admitted. "I agree with the sentiment, but I can't seem to stay away from them these days."

"It's not your fault," Emma said. "You haven't had anything you could turn your back on. I'm just sorry I can't help. If I try to do anything again, Dad said he's sending me to my aunt Tess's, and trust me, that's incentive enough to keep on the straight and narrow."

"You don't like your aunt?"

"She's not really my aunt; she's an old family friend. The woman is pushing ninety, and she still drives, though not often, and certainly not well. Even with all that, it's still better than her cooking. You wouldn't believe some of the things she's tried to get me to eat in the past."

"Then it's a good idea to stay out of this," I said. I was overprotective of Emma, and I tried to keep her involvement in my impromptu investigations to a minimum, though she usually protested the exclusion.

"There is one thing I can tell you that shouldn't break his rule," Emma said.

"Are you sure?"

She grinned at me in the near darkness.

The only light we had was from the donut shop window behind us, and that was coming through the open kitchen door. "There's just one way to find out. It's about Lacy Newman."

"What about her?" I asked. So much for not getting her involved.

"Dad thinks Lacy had plenty of motive to want Lester to come to harm."

"Was the editorial he was going to do on Lacy really that bad?"

Emma nodded. "Evidently. She's got some secret she's hiding from the world, and Lester was going to expose it."

"Does your dad know what the secret was?"

Emma shrugged. "It's got something to do with her late husband. That's all he knows. Want me to dig into it a little?"

"No," I said a little too loudly.

"I was just asking," Emma said defensively.

In a calmer voice, I said, "We don't want you to go to your aunt's, do we?"

"You're right. Forget I said anything," Emma said.

Our break was almost over, and as I led the way back inside, I said, "Thanks for the tip, Emma."

"I just wish I could do more."

I hugged her. "Just keep helping me make donuts, and we're good," I said.

By ten o'clock, we'd had a decent flow of customers, but there was no word from Jake or George yet. I'd hoped to at least see one of them, and if I had to choose, it wouldn't come as a surprise to anyone that I'd pick Jake. Having him in town and not being able to be with him was enough to drive me crazy. Maybe I'd be able to talk him into dinner at Napoli's in Union Square if I promised not to discuss murder while we were there. It was worth a try, so as soon as there was a lull, I grabbed my cell phone and dialed his number. It went straight to voice mail, so I said, "Hey, it's me. Let's have dinner tonight and forget about the outside world. How does Napoli's sound? Call me. Oh, and this is Suzanne."

I don't know why I added the last bit, but I was pretty sure it would make him smile, and who needed more reason than that?

I was still feeling good about the invitation when an older woman walked in with a perpetual frown on her face.

"May I help you?" I asked, doing my best to not let her ruin my good mood.

"I need to see the owner," she snapped.

"I'm Suzanne Hart. What can I do for you?"

She looked me up and down twice, and then said, "I think it's disgraceful what you're doing."

What an odd thing to say. "What in particular have I done?"

Her frown deepened. "Don't play dumb with me. I know you're dating a priest. Shame on you."

"Pardon me?" I was honestly shocked by her accusation. We got unusual customers from time to time, but this woman went well beyond eccentric. I'd almost rather have had the clown back.

"You're dating a priest."

Then it dawned on me. "Not priest, Bishop," I said.

I was about to explain that it was my boyfriend's last name and not his job title when she said, "That's even worse."

She stormed off before I even had a chance to explain.

Life could be interesting dealing with the public; there was no doubt about that.

It was just past eleven and the shop was fairly empty when the mayor came into the donut store, an unexpected visit, since he didn't normally frequent my place.

"What can I get you?" I asked.

He looked at the cases. "I'll take four dozen donuts, your choice."

What had brought that on? I wasn't sure, but I wasn't going to protest. I could use the business.

As I boxed them, I asked, "Any reason in particular?"

"I'm doing a talk at the senior center, and I thought I'd bring treats with me. I never stop running for reelection. It's the nature of the beast."

"I can imagine," I said as I boxed the donuts. It put a healthy hole in my inventory, and maybe I wouldn't have to give any donuts away today. That would be a nice feeling, for a change of pace.

He handed me a fifty, and as I started to count out what he had coming back to him, Cam smiled at me. "Keep the change."

"I can't keep a tip that's more than the donuts cost," I said.

"I insist. It's my way of taking care of one of our valuable small businesses in town. The way I see it, helping you is just helping myself."

Was he really trying to curry favor with me by bribing me? It would take a great deal more than that to buy my loyalty. He started to take the boxes, but I put one hand on the stack and grabbed his change out of the till with the other. I put the money on top, and then released my grip.

The mayor frowned. "Are you saying my money's not good enough for you, Suzanne?"

"No," I said evenly. "I'll take all the money you're willing to spend, but I won't take any as a tip for doing my job. You should understand that better than anyone."

"What do you mean by that?" he asked pointedly.

"I'm not accusing you of anything. All I'm saying is that I don't think it's my place as the owner to accept gratuities." At least not from you, I added silently to myself.

"So that's the way it's going to be, is it?" He looked at the donuts, and then said, "You know what? I've changed my mind."

"Sorry, no refunds," I said as I tapped the sign on the back of my register. I'd put it there to discourage people trying to get half-donuts from me, and now I was glad I'd done it.

"Fine," he said, losing his politician's cool for a moment before taking the money on top and shoving it in his pocket.

As he picked up the boxes, I asked, "May I get the door for you?"

"I'll manage," he said as he pushed his

way out. I almost wished he'd drop one or two, though I couldn't stand the thought of wasting any of my donuts.

I heard laughing when he was gone, and looked over at the only customer left in the shop, Elizabeth Boone. Elizabeth was a sweet older woman who allowed herself one donut a week, and she savored it as though it were made of gold. "I'm afraid he's not a fan of yours, Suzanne."

"Was I too rough on him?" I asked.

"I think it was perfect. If you ask me, Cam Hamilton always was a little too slick for our little town. After he shakes my hand, I always count my fingers to make sure they add up to five."

I laughed in response, and Elizabeth quickly added, "I shouldn't have said that. It must be the donut talking."

"If they ever do that, I'm running for the hills," I said. "You made my day. Can I get you another donut, on the house?"

She looked sorely tempted before saying, "I'd love to, but who knows where that might lead? Two today, and then three when I come by next week. After that, I start having some every day, and before I know it, I'll never fit into the dress I want to wear to my reunion." Elizabeth paused, then said, "I must sound like a batty old woman."

"You make perfect sense. I just wish I had your willpower. I have a hard time not sampling the wares here."

Elizabeth smiled. "I don't know how you do it. I'd weigh five hundred pounds if I had to deal with the temptations you face every day. Thanks for the offer, though."

"You're welcome."

I was about to close, with still no sign of George or Jake, when Sherry Lance came in the door. What was going on?

"Can I get you something? If you came to collect on my donut offer, I'm happy to oblige you."

She shook her head. "I don't have time for pleasantries. Did you have a fight with the mayor today?"

"I wouldn't exactly call it a fight," I said. "We had a few words, but neither one of us raised our voice. Why do you ask?"

"I just found out that he wants the county health inspector to do an emergency inspection here."

"I've got nothing to hide," I said, hoping that was true. I prided myself on my cleanliness, but I also knew that if an inspector had a grudge, he could easily find something wrong with any kitchen. "How did you find out?"

"I was at city hall doing some paperwork

when I heard him on the phone. Be careful, Suzanne. I know he strikes a lot of people as a glad-hander, but Cam's got a bite to go along with his bark."

"I'll watch my back," I said. "Thanks for the warning."

She shrugged as she put a hand on the door. "I just don't like bullies. I never have. If I can help you in any way, just let me know."

"I will."

After she was gone, I was a little more shaken than I would have liked to admit. I knew Cam hadn't been happy with me, but what would make him overreact like that? Had I said something that hit a nerve about taking a gratuity for doing my job? Was it possible he'd once taken a bribe to make something happen, and his guilty conscience had caused him to come after me now? If he was trying to scare me off, he was going to fail. I'd have to mention what happened to Jake and George to get their reactions to his behavior. In the meantime, I needed to make sure the place was as clean as humanly possible. I locked the front door, even though we still had a few minutes, and flipped the sign.

Emma was doing the last batch of dishes in back when I joined her. Her iPod must have been turned up high, because when I tapped her shoulder, she nearly jumped out of her shoes. "Don't sneak up on me like that," she said.

"Turn it down and I won't be able to. We need to stay a little late today."

She looked crestfallen. "Today? Really? We didn't get any special orders, did we?"

"No, but it's time for a thorough cleaning. Did you have plans?"

"Nothing set in stone," she said.

"If you have a date for lunch, you don't have to stay."

"No, I'll help."

I smiled at her. "Good. I'll pay you time and a half, and you can afford to take him out to dinner instead."

"I'll do it. He'll like that."

That was news, since I'd been kidding. "I didn't realize you had anybody in your life at the moment."

Emma grinned at me. "You know me. I love falling in love."

"What's his name?"

"Does it matter?" she asked with a smile. "I don't think he'll last long, but for now, we're having fun together, and that's all that counts."

"Just be careful," I said.

"Yes, Mom," she replied with a smile.

"Why the rush cleaning job?"

"Let's just say I want to be prepared for anything that might happen."

We were still cleaning when I heard a knock on the front door. If it was the health inspector, we were in trouble. Emma and I needed another hour before the place would be pristine, and I wasn't sure how I could talk my way out of this one.

Thankfully, when I peeked around the corner, I saw Grace standing there trying to look inside.

I unlocked the door. "Come on in."

"Are you ready to go?"

"No, we're cleaning. Want to lend a hand?"

"Why not?" she asked, surprising me. Grace was many things, but a thorough cleaner was not one of them. "What can I do to help?"

I still had two dozen donuts left I had to get rid of. "If you could give these away, I'd appreciate it."

"Should I take them to the church?"

"No," I said, "they asked me to take a little break. I've had so many left lately, they're getting tired of them. Be creative."

"I can do that," she said.

I let her out, then rejoined Emma. "Let's shift into turbo," I said.

"I'm game if you are."

As we cleaned, I kept trying to think of things that Grace could do once she got back, but the longer we worked, the less of an issue it became. A part of me wondered what she could possibly be doing, but I was also glad that Emma and I weren't interrupted anymore. By the time we finished, Donut Hearts was ready for a white-glove inspection.

I let Emma go, and then locked the door. Grace was twenty feet away, with one empty box at her feet and the other open. "What exactly are you doing?"

"I'm giving away samples. It's not as easy as you'd think."

I laughed as I looked into the box and found a few old-fashioned inside. "I think it's safe to throw those away. You didn't have to do that."

"It was fun," she said. "What was the big cleaning rush?"

"I had a run-in with the mayor. I didn't think much about it, but Sherry came by and warned me that he was trying to get me shut down with a health inspection."

"Wow, what did you say to him?"

"I implied that you shouldn't take a gift for doing your job."

Grace laughed. "When you stir the pot,

you really put some muscle into it, don't you?"

"You know me. I don't do anything half-way."

"Any donuts left in there?" a voice said behind me.

I turned around and said, "Where have you been all day? I've been waiting for you."

# CHAPTER 12

George smiled as he took one of the last donuts and ate it. "Investigating is hard work. It's easy to build up an appetite," he said with a smile. "Besides, I didn't say when I'd check in with you. What's going on?"

I brought him up to speed, and when I told him about Cam's overreaction, he said, "I've heard rumors about him, but I didn't think there was anything to it. How does it tie into Lester, though?"

"Could Cam have been afraid that Lester was about to expose him for the library property sale?"

George frowned. "If Lester had had the slightest shred of proof, he'd have gone after Cam instead of airing a donut diatribe the night he died."

"I don't know, but I must have put some kind of fear into him," I said.

"Watch your back, Suzanne."

"You're the second person who's told me to do that today."

"It makes sense that Jake would want you to be careful," he said.

"Not Jake. It was Sherry Lance."

George whistled as he retrieved the last donut. "It sounds like you're making a lot more headway than I am."

"Why? What have you found out?"

"Not enough to even be worth reporting. That's what's taken me so long to get back to you. I haven't had much luck at all."

"Cheer up," I said as I patted his shoulder. "It's not a race."

"Good, because I'd be losing." He waved the donut in the air, and then said, "See you later. I'd tell you both to stay out of trouble, but why waste my breath?"

I grinned back at him. "You're smarter than you look."

"And isn't that a good thing."

After he was gone, I took the empty boxes from Grace and threw them away.

She followed me to the trash can, and then asked, "Any ideas about what we should do next?"

"I want to head to Union Square and talk to Nancy Patton again. I'm not satisfied with her responses to our questions."

"Sounds good."

We were heading for my Jeep when Gabby Williams called out from her secondhand clothing store, ReNEWed.

"Ladies, we need to talk," Gabby said.

That was never a good sign, even on my best day.

"We were just on our way out," I said. "Is it important?"

"Would I delay you if it weren't?" Gabby was a trim woman in her fifties, but whether she was on the high end or the low was cause for much speculation since she'd come to town. She had her finger on the pulse of April Springs, her secondhand shop allowing her to mine information from all walks of life, and even though she was a valuable resource, I wasn't all that keen on tapping it. There was a fine line between Gabby's friends and her enemies, and it wasn't in my best interests to ever cross it, though I'd pushed the boundaries a time or two in the past.

She clearly wasn't about to take no for an answer, though. "Let's have some tea while we talk."

I looked at Grace, who shrugged and then nodded. "Tea sounds lovely." Grace had gotten on Gabby's bad side somehow, and she was doing her best to make amends.

Gabby smiled. "Excellent. It's ready now,

so we won't have to wait."

We walked into her shop, and I was amazed yet again by how orderly the place was. If I didn't know the clothes she offered were used, I'd be hard-pressed to swear one way or the other. Some of her things were from town, but a great many more came from some mysterious supplier out of town. I wasn't sure I wanted to know any more than that. It was odd how many secondhand shops I'd visited lately. Didn't anyone ever buy anything new anymore?

In back, Gabby had her tea service waiting for us. It was clear she'd been watching Donut Hearts in anticipation of our departure. Whatever she had to say, she considered it important.

We sat, and Gabby served.

"What's this brew?" I asked as I took my cup. It was excellent.

"It's a personal blend I had made up especially for me," she said proudly.

"Well, it's great," I said.

"Thank you. You two are looking into Lester Moorefield's murder." As she said it, her stare shifted from me to Grace, and then back again.

When neither one of us commented, Gabby added, "Are either one of you going to answer me?"

"I didn't realize there was a question in there," I said. "We are, and you can imagine why I'm eager to have his murderer caught. I don't want one of my pastries blamed for killing him, and I especially don't want the pastry maker to be blamed."

"That suspicion has hurt business already, hasn't it?"

I looked up from my tea. "How could you possibly know that?"

Gabby laughed. "Suzanne, our businesses are close together. Did you think for one moment I wouldn't keep an eye on street traffic?"

"I suppose not," I replied. I glanced over at Grace, who was sipping her tea and not saying a word. It was the wisest course of action, but one I'd never been able to take myself, no matter the circumstances.

Gabby patted my hand. "We are women who own businesses in a small Southern town. It is in our best interests to watch out for each other."

"Thanks," I said, meaning it. It was nice having her in my corner, even if we weren't best friends.

"So, who is on that list of yours so far?"

Grace, contributing to her own downfall, chose that moment to speak. "I thought you were giving out information, not collecting it."

The stare Gabby gave her was enough to melt stone, and Grace realized that she'd overstepped her bounds.

"Is there any reason I can't, or shouldn't, do both?"

Grace was quick to apologize. "I didn't mean anything by it. I'm just so curious about what you know."

If Gabby was mollified by the explanation, she didn't show it. She looked expectantly at me, and I knew I might as well tell her who we thought was involved so far.

"So far, we've got Lacy Newman, Cam Hamilton, Sherry Lance, a builder named Vern Yancey, Nancy Patton, and Cara Lassiter."

Gabby nodded as I shared each name on the list. "I'm familiar with all of them except Nancy Patton."

"She was Lester's wife," I said.

"What?" Gabby gasped out, nearly choking on her tea. "He was married?"

"You didn't know?" I asked, trying my best not to act smug that I'd found out something she didn't know.

She shook her head. "I'm sorry, but we have to cut this short. I've got a migraine headache, and it's suddenly killing me."

I couldn't let her go just like that, though. "What was your information? I shared all I know with you."

Gabby walked us to the front of the store, and as she let us out, she said, "Lacy's got a secret she's been protecting for a dozen years, and I heard that Lester was going to reveal it. It could be a sound motive for murder. Now if you'll excuse me, I'm going to go home and lie down."

"I hope your headache gets better," I said as she nearly shoved us out the door.

"What was that all about?" I asked as Grace and I walked to my Jeep.

"She nearly choked when she heard about Lester's wife. It was almost funny knowing something that she didn't."

"There was more to it than that, Grace. The news disturbed her so much she didn't even try to make up a good excuse to kick us out. Gabby must have had a reason to be upset, but I don't have the slightest idea what it could be." A thought so ridiculous it didn't bear being spoken aloud occurred to me. I dismissed it instantly, but Grace must have been watching me.

"What?" she asked.

"Excuse me?"

"You had an idea, but then you killed it. I want to know what you were thinking."

"It's crazy," I answered.

"Then it should fit right in with us."

After a moment's hesitation, I asked, "Is there any way Lester and Gabby were dating?"

Grace shook her head. "Thanks a lot. I won't be able to get that image out of my head now. You're right. It's crazy."

"I told you."

Grace took another step, and then said, "It does make sense, though. She reacted to the news that Lester had been married a lot more strongly than she should have."

"We need to find out if it could be true," I said. "If they were dating, she might have had some reason for wanting him dead."

"I know I'd feel that way if I was going out with Lester," Grace said.

"We need to forget it for now. It's time to speak with Lacy," I said, then noticed Grace hesitate at the Jeep door. "Something wrong?"

"I'm not sure how I'm going to interrogate an old lady I like," she admitted.

"You don't have to come along. I can do it by myself."

Grace shook her head and climbed into the Jeep. "No, if you're doing it, then I am, too. Have you thought about how you're going to handle it?"

"I thought I might give the straightforward approach another try," I said as I started the Jeep.

"You're a rebel investigator; you know that, don't you?"

"It's too tough to hide why we're asking questions of our friends," I admitted, "but don't give up all hope. I'm certain we can fool someone with a cover story before this is all over."

"I'll be disappointed if we don't at least try," she said with a grin. Part of the reason Grace liked to help me were the outlandish stories we created to get the information we were after. There were times I worried that she didn't take things seriously enough, but all in all, she was a good person to have watching my back.

Lacy was working in her garden when we drove up. I couldn't believe how she'd managed to make her flowers bloom so beautifully. Momma and I had tried to grow a hummingbird and butterfly garden in the backyard of our cottage, with minimal success. It might be the perfect lead-in for asking questions. As I stopped in the street in front of her place, I told Grace, "Follow my lead."

"Are we going to try to trick Lacy? Suzanne, she's known us our entire lives."

"I'm going to ask the questions. If you'd like, you can sit in the Jeep."

"I'll come with you," she said as she got out. Grace wasn't afraid of anything or anyone, but it seemed she didn't want to offend Lacy at any cost. I'd have to find out why, but this wasn't a good time to do it. I had questions to ask, starting easy, and ending up hard.

"I love your flowers," I said as we approached. "Grace and I were driving past, and we just had to stop to admire them."

Lacy's eyes softened when she saw Grace. "How are you, child?"

"I'm fine, ma'am," she said.

"Tell me your secret," I said. "Momma and I have been trying to do something like this, on a smaller scale, and we've raised more weeds than flowers."

Lacy smiled. "I'm sure you're exaggerating."

"I only wish I were," I said.

Lacy nodded. "I strip the grass from a new spot where I want my garden, then I take a shovel and turn the soil. After that, I rake it smooth."

"That's all it takes?" I asked, interrupting her.

"That's barely the beginning. Next I lay

down four thicknesses of newsprint, add a pickup truck full of topsoil from Hardy's Garden Center, and mix in two bushels of horse manure. It's gold to a real gardener."

"It sounds like a lot of work," I said.

"Oh, it is, but the results justify the commitment. Arthur always thought so, at any rate."

Arthur was her late husband, and if the rumors were to be believed, he was the secret Lacy was hiding. "I never really knew him," I admitted. "How did he die?"

"His heart stopped," she said simply.

"I suppose that's what ultimately happens to all of us," I said, not realizing how it might sound to Lacy.

Grace snapped, "Suzanne, that was uncalled for."

Lacy shook her head before I could reply. "Easy, Grace, she didn't mean anything by it. Isn't that what happens to us all, eventually?" As she spoke, Lacy kept moving the weeding tool in her hand, flicking out and removing the offending plants with great ease. I watched her, thinking that while Lacy might look frail, her hands were certainly strong enough to strangle someone, especially if she caught them by surprise.

"I'm sorry," I said. "I didn't intend to be

insensitive. I understand Lester Moorefield was coming after you next."

A look of distaste crossed her face. "What a dreadful, petty little man. I heard his attack on your donuts."

"I hate to admit it, but there was a seed of truth in what he said," I replied. "From what I've been hearing, he was going to be even harder on you."

For a split second, Lacy's smile faltered, but it was back so quickly that I began to doubt what I'd seen. "That man certainly had an imagination, I'll give him that."

"Donuts were my sin," I said, trying to keep my voice light. "What was yours going to be?"

Grace started to say something, and I warned her off with a quick glare. This was what we'd been leading up to all along.

Lacy made another stab at the ground with her tool, and then said, "I'm tired. I'm afraid I need to go in now. It was nice seeing you both."

Once she was gone, Grace asked, "What did you think you were doing? You practically accused her of murder."

I looked carefully at my best friend. "Grace, what are you not telling me?"

"I don't know what you're talking about, Suzanne," she said.

Something was troubling her, that was certain. "Come on, we've been friends nearly our entire lives. Whatever it is, you can trust me."

"You wouldn't understand," she said, her voice quivering a little as she spoke.

"Try me. I'm on your side. You know that. No matter what."

Grace looked as though she wanted to cry, and I felt like a real heel, but I had to know what hold Lacy had over her.

After nearly a minute, my friend said, "When I was younger, my parents were fighting all the time, and I had nowhere to go. I could only stay at your house so long, you know. You had your own life. One night when you were out of town, my parents had a horrible fight, and I had to get out. I ran away from home, and I happened to walk by Lacy's. She was out on her porch, saw my tears, and called me to her. We spoke for hours about everything under the sun, and by bedtime, I was ready to go home. But not alone. Lacy walked me to the front porch, then went inside to speak with my parents while I waited there. I don't know what she said, but all I know is they stopped fighting in front of me after that. I owe Lacy more than I could ever repay for standing up for me." Grace was crying as she spoke, and I hugged her quickly.

"Why didn't you ever tell me about it?" I asked when she was a little calmer.

"I was ashamed of them," she admitted, "and myself."

"I'll try to be gentler with her from now on," I said, "but I can't just let this go. You know that, don't you?"

"I do," she said. "I don't think I can come back here with you again, though. It's just too hard on me."

"I understand completely. Do you want to stop for the day, or do you feel like going somewhere else with me?"

"That depends," she said as we got into the Jeep. "Where did you have in mind?"

"I thought we'd head over to Union Square and talk to Nancy Patton again. I'm not going to leave this time until I get a confession or an alibi I can prove. What do you say? Are you with me?"

"Don't worry; I have no problem ganging up on her," she said with a smile.

We were parked and heading into Nancy Patton's business when I saw a familiar car nearby.

"It might not be a bad idea to put this off," I said.

"Why?" Grace asked. "You're not getting

cold feet about questioning one of our suspects now, are you?"

I pointed at Jake's car. "With him in there, I do. We could always pop in to Napoli's and get a quick bite."

"We've already cadged one meal out of them. Let's try somewhere else."

"Why would you want to do that?" Jake asked as he stepped toward us. "You love Napoli's." I'd just assumed he'd been in Nancy's shop, so I hadn't expected him to be across the street. Evidently he'd gotten close enough to hear some of what we'd said. "What brings you two to town?"

"Would you believe me if I said we came here looking for you?" I asked.

That got a soft chuckle. "Not on your life. You're here to grill Ms. Patton, so don't try to deny it. It just makes you look desperate."

I smiled at him. "You caught us." I extended my wrists. "Would you like to lock us both up?"

"Don't tempt me," he replied with a grin of his own, and then turned to Grace. "I see she's roped you in on another investigation."

"I just can't seem to say no," Grace answered. "Why don't I take a walk down the street so you two can have some privacy."

I said, "Thanks," at the same time Jake said, "No need."

Grace looked at us both, and then said, "See? You can't even agree on that."

Before either one of us could say another word, Grace took off.

"What was that all about?" I asked Jake. "You're not avoiding me, are you?"

"If I were, it would be to protect you."

That answer surprised me. "From what?"

"Wagging tongues mostly, but ultimately, from yourself."

"Don't worry about me; I can take care of myself," I answered.

"Okay then, do it for my sake."

"You can handle things even better than I can," I admitted.

"Let's just say my job's easier if the people I'm investigating don't know about our relationship."

I frowned at him. "I've got to admit, I don't like that. You're not ashamed to be seen with me, are you?"

"Are you kidding? I love it. It just makes things too complicated sometimes."

"Then I guess Napoli's is out for tonight."

He shrugged. "Sorry, it's a little too public, given the investigation."

"I want to see you," I said a little more emphatically than I should have. "Tell you what. Why don't you come by the house and Momma and I will feed you. You can even park in the lot and walk across the grass to our place. Nobody has to know you're even there."

"I don't have to be that clandestine," he answered.

"Let's not take any chances. How does six sound to you?"

"Great, if you're sure I'm not putting you out."

I laughed. "You know my mother. She'll be delighted to have you, and I shouldn't have to tell you how I feel." I pointed to the consignment shop. "Have you spoken with her yet?"

Jake nodded, the frown lines showing in his face. "She's a hard woman, isn't she? To be honest with you, I didn't have much luck."

"Maybe Grace and I will do better."

"I suppose stranger things have happened."

"Thanks for the vote of confidence," I said with a slight grin.

"Suzanne, we both know that confidence is one thing you don't lack."

"What's another?" I asked.

"I could stand here complimenting you all day, but I have work to do. See you tonight."

"Tonight it is."

# CHAPTER 13

I hadn't planned on conducting the interview without Grace, but I wasn't about to let an opportunity when there were no customers go to waste. It was time to ask Nancy some tough questions.

"We need to talk," I said as I walked inside and approached her.

"I did all my talking with him," she answered. "If he struck out, do you honestly think I'd talk to you?" I could see Jake through the window, and Nancy kept staring at him until he got into his car and drove out of our line of sight. "I saw you two talking out there. What did he want with you?"

"You're not the only one he's giving a hard time to," I said. "I figured you might want to help me get him off both our backs."

"How can you do that?"

At least I had her interest. Apparently Jake's questioning had bothered her more than she'd wanted to let on. "Tell me what

I need to know, and I can sic him on somebody else's tail."

"Why would you do that for me?" This woman didn't trust anyone.

I shrugged. "By helping you, I help myself. I really just have one question for you. Do you have an alibi for the night Lester was murdered?"

"I was with someone."

"Did you tell the state police inspector that?"

Nancy bit her lower lip for a second. "It's complicated. He's married, and his wife's the jealous type."

After what I'd been through with my ex-husband, Max, I wasn't especially fond of cheaters, but I needed this woman on my side. "Call him, tell him it's okay to talk to me, and I can convince the police that you couldn't have done it." I'd been about to say that she was innocent, but clearly that would be a stretch.

"Hang on," Nancy said, and excused herself. As she walked into the back room to make her telephone call, I had to wonder who this mystery man was. Would he come forward to alibi her, or would he leave her dangling in the wind and move on to his next conquest? Momma always said that if a man cheats with you, someday he'll cheat on you. I know for a fact that she hadn't been talking directly about Max, since he'd been unattached when we got together, but I had to wonder if she sensed something about the man that love had blinded me to. I wouldn't be the first woman it had ever happened to, and I doubted that I would be the last.

I was still musing about that when Nancy came back in. "Sorry, I can't help you. He's out of town at the moment."

Convenient, I thought, but did not say. In three seconds, I was glad I'd managed to keep my mouth shut, because Nancy added, "He'll be by the donut shop sometime tomorrow, and he'll back me up."

"I'm free now," I said, hating to leave any loose ends hanging. "I'll meet him wherever he might be."

"Chicago?" she asked. "He's away on business and won't be back until late to-night. It's that, or nothing."

"I'll take that," I said. "Who should I look for?"

"Don't worry, he'll find you there."

A tour bus must have stopped outside, because a gaggle of shoppers came in together, ogling the sights. I recognized the expression on Nancy's face as one of my own. Business could be like that sometimes.

Things were slow and uneventful for what seemed like forever, and then, all of sudden, you had more work than you could handle.

I left her as she tried to watch every person in her shop at the same time, and found Grace outside eating an ice cream cone.

"That looks good," I said.

"There's plenty more right over there," she answered as she pointed to a shop nearby. "I was wondering where you went, and then I spotted you inside. You were in such an earnest conversation with Nancy that I didn't want to interrupt. Find out anything good?"

"She's got an alibi."

"Then we can mark her off our list."

"It's not that simple," I explained. "He's a married man, and she wouldn't give me his name."

"So, she stays on the list."

"For now. He's supposed to come by Donut Hearts sometime tomorrow to confirm her alibi."

"I bet Jake's going to just love that." She looked around and noticed that his car was gone. "What happened? You didn't run him off, did you?"

"No, he had to go. We're having dinner tonight, though."

Grace's eyes lit up. "Where's he taking you? Someplace nice, I hope."

"Momma and I are cooking for him," I admitted. "Speaking of which, I'd better call and give her a heads-up."

"You can do it on the way back to April Springs," Grace said.

"It'll just take a second." I dialed my home number, and Momma answered. "Hey, it's me."

"Hello, me."

"What's for dinner?"

"I was thinking we could rob the freezer and have another leftover night. Why?"

I tried not to laugh as I said, "That sounds good. I invited Jake over, and I'm sure he'd love to scrounge through your freezer with the two of us."

That perked her up instantly. "Nonsense. Let's see, is there time for a roast? When exactly is he coming?"

"Six," I answered.

"No time for that, then. Don't worry, I'll come up with something grand."

"Momma, no offense, but I don't think he's coming strictly for the cooking. At least I hope not."

"Suzanne, leave the menu to me. When will you be home?"

"I'm in Union Square, so it might be a

while," I admitted.

"Excellent."

"You're happy that I'm out of town?" What an odd reaction to get from my own mother.

"No, just that you're there. Before you come back, I need you to swing by Olson's and pick up a few things."

"Grace is here with me, too, Momma." If I could get out of making the shopping trip, I was going to.

"She can help, as well. Do you have a pen and paper handy?"

I mimed to Grace a pencil writing, and she dove into her purse and pulled them both out. I normally confined myself to a wallet or a small handbag, but Grace liked to be prepared for anything short of the end of the world.

"Go on," I said, and I wrote as quickly as I could to keep up with her. After she was finished, I asked sarcastically, "Is that all?"

"No, but I already have the rest of what I need. You can invite Grace, too, if you'd like. The more the merrier."

"While we're at it, she can include twelve of her closest friends, too. That's a lot of food."

"Nonsense. The man doesn't get to eat home cooking very often."

243

After I hung up, I said, "I guess you heard we're going shopping."

She was grinning broadly at me. "She didn't exactly give you a chance to say no, did she? Don't worry about it, Suzanne. I can pick up a few things myself while we're here."

It appeared that my investigation, at least for now, was over.

I was out of the shower and toweling off my hair when my cell phone rang. If it was Jake canceling, I was going to skin him alive. Momma had pulled out all of the stops, making chicken *and* meat loaf, with garlic mashed potatoes, creamed spinach, candied carrots, and sweet potato casserole. I'd tried to help until I kept getting in her way and she finally sent me upstairs to take a shower and get the smell of donuts out of my hair. I could never be entirely successful, since the scent felt permanent sometimes, but I could do my best to disguise the scent with mango or strawberry. Jake claimed he loved the smell of fried donuts, but I knew he could just be trying to mollify me.

I saw that it wasn't Jake when I picked it up.

"I've been wondering if you'd call," I said to George after saying hello. "Any progress on your poking around into Lester's life?"

"I'm pursuing something even as we speak," he said cryptically.

"Anything in particular?"

"Positively," he said.

"Care to share?" Why was he being so mysterious all of a sudden?

"I can't," he said. "If I'm wrong, I could ruin someone's reputation, and I can't bring myself to do that to someone who might be innocent."

"I won't tell anyone," I said. "You know you can trust me."

He started to say something, I could feel it in my bones, when he suddenly went silent. "Come on, you know you want to," I added, trying to convince him to talk.

"Maybe tomorrow," he said. "If not then, the next day for sure."

"You're not taking any chances, are you?"

"What's life without taking a risk now and then," he said. I could almost hear him smiling over the telephone.

"George, please be careful. If something happens to you while you're helping me out, I'll never be able to forgive myself. I mean it."

That sobered him. "Suzanne, I'll be as careful as I can, given the circumstances. This might be the break we need to solve

Lester's murder."

I started to say something when he cut me off. "Gotta go. They're back."

"Who's back? George? Are you there?"

I was talking into a dead phone.

Why did that man insist on taking so many chances? He missed being a cop, putting his life on the line every day. Was helping me just an excuse to feed his adrenaline habit? Was I enabling him somehow? I wouldn't be able to stop worrying about him until I knew he was safe.

My phone rang again, and I didn't even look at the caller ID as I grabbed it. "George? Are you okay?"

"It's me," Jake said. "What's wrong with George?"

"Nothing," I answered, not able to come up with anything on the spot.

"Suzanne," Jake said.

"He's doing something for me, and I wanted to be sure he was okay."

I could hear Jake take a deep breath, and then slowly let it out. "Do I want to know what he's doing?"

"I sincerely doubt it," I answered as honestly as I could. "I don't even know myself, so there's no use grilling me about it."

"Okay, forget I asked. I've got some bad news."

"You're not canceling on us, are you? Momma went to a lot of trouble to make dinner tonight."

"No, it's not that. I'm just running a little late."

Maybe I could let him live after all. "How late?"

"Half an hour," he answered.

"Ten minutes? That shouldn't be too bad."

"I get it," he said. "I'll try my best to shave it to that."

"You'd better. Trust me, you don't want to miss this meal."

"I'll be there. Don't start without me."

I laughed. "I'll try, but I'm not making any promises."

"Then I'd better go," he said as he hung up.

As I got dressed, I couldn't help wondering what was delaying him. Did it have something to do with the case, or was it something else? I'd been dying to ask, but I was afraid of what his answer might be.

I came down promptly at six to find Momma waiting at the bottom of the stairs for me. "You took your sweet time, Suzanne. He's due here any minute."

"Actually, he's going to be late. He called,

but I forgot to tell you. Sorry about that."

"Any idea how long he'll be delayed?"

"He started with half an hour, but I got him down to ten minutes."

"Did he say what was delaying him?"

"He didn't offer any information, and I didn't ask," I said as I walked into the dining room. We were eating formally tonight, and Momma had outdone herself, both on the food selections and the table settings. I leaned down and kissed the top of her head. "Thanks for doing this."

"It's my pleasure, and you know it."

"Sure I do, but it's still nice to thank you."

"You're most welcome. Would you like me to make up a plate and take it to my room? I'd be happy to give you both some privacy."

I couldn't help laughing at the thought of my mother teetering on the edge of her bed trying to cut up her chicken without sending the plate spilling to the floor. "If you do, I'm eating in my room, too. You could always make up a doggy bag for Jake, but I don't know where he's going to eat his meal."

"I thought I'd offer."

Nine minutes later, the doorbell rang.

I threw the front door open, and saw Jake standing there with a bouquet of flowers. "For me? They're beautiful."

"They are," he agreed, but made no move to deliver them to me. "They're also not for you."

"I'm not sure I like you bringing another woman flowers," I said.

"That's an excellent point. Next time I'll bring two," he replied.

"I suppose that will have to do. She's going to love them."

Momma called out from the kitchen, "Suzanne, are you going to let him inside?"

"You need to come out here," I said to her.

My mother poked her head out. "Why is that? I'm putting the finishing touches on this gravy."

"He brought you flowers," I said.

"The gravy can wait, then," she answered as she came out.

Jake presented them to her, and then said, "Thanks for inviting me, Dorothy."

"Very good. You didn't even stutter that time. You're always welcome." She handed the flowers to me and said, "Suzanne, put these in water."

"Yes, ma'am," I said, taking them from her. It was awfully thoughtful of him, and I knew he was scoring big points with my mother. I just hoped he didn't forget to score a few with me, as well.

"That smells wonderful," he said.

"Let's go enjoy it, shall we?" Momma answered.

We went into the dining room and sat at the table. The feast was laid out, and Momma said, "You two sit, and I'll be right back."

Once she was gone, Jake looked at the spread and asked, "Who else is coming? This is enough to feed an army."

"Don't worry, what we don't eat, we'll freeze. Some of my momma's best meals are leftovers."

"I can believe that."

While we had a few minutes, I asked, "What kept you, anyway?"

He glanced at his watch. "Hey, I promised ten minutes, and I made it in nine. I can't do much better than that."

"Did you get a break in the case?"

"I can't talk about that, and you shouldn't ask."

His voice was flat, his words devoid of emotion. I'd crossed the line we'd agreed to respect.

"I'm sorry," I said immediately. "I was out of line. Can we forget it happened?"

Jake seemed to think about it, and then said, "If you forgive me for not bringing you flowers, too, we can call it even."

I stuck my hand out to him. "Deal."

He stood, leaned over, and kissed me. A second later, he said, "I'd rather seal it that way myself."

"I hope you don't do that with all of your agreements," I said. As I looked up, I saw Momma standing in the doorway. Was that a smile on her face? How much of what had happened had she witnessed?

"Is everyone ready to eat?" she asked.

"More than ready," Jake answered.

As we enjoyed her fine food, I did my best to be charming, even coming close to matching Momma's natural social graces. I'd pushed Jake for information when I had no right, and I was bound and determined to make up for it by being as pleasant as I could be.

After the meal, Momma said, "It's a beautiful night. Why don't you two take a stroll in the park? When you come back, I'll have pie for you."

"What kind did you make?" Jake asked.

I laughed and nudged him gently. "Could you honestly eat another bite? You were a marvel the way you tore through that dinner."

"Suzanne," my mother said, employing her motherly voice again.

"It's fine, ma'am," Jake said. "She's right,

but I've had your pie before, remember? I think if I took a walk around the park, I might be able to handle a slice." He turned to me and asked, "What do you think? Are you game?"

"I am if you are," I said. "Why don't you go ahead? I want to help with the dishes."

Momma wasn't hearing any of that, though. "Nonsense. Go on, both of you."

There was no use arguing with her, and I knew it. "Let's go, Jake. We can't win this one. Trust me, I've got years of experience."

"We'll see you soon, then," Jake said.

As we walked out onto the porch, he said to me, "Suzanne, I need to do more for your mother than give her flowers. She's a real treasure."

"What can I say? Like mother, like daughter."

"I'm serious. Is there anything I can do to repay her for the kindness she continually shows me?"

"Take good care of her daughter," I said in all seriousness.

"I already do that, don't I?"

I kissed him, and then pulled away, smiling. "Okay, I'll give you that one. I'll think about it and get back to you."

"I'm serious about this."

"So am I. Now let's take that walk so you

can get your pie."

As we walked around the park, past my favorite hiding place, my thinking place, and the Patriot's Tree, I marveled about how good Jake's hand felt holding mine. I was glad we'd forgone a dinner out and had stayed home. Being with him there was what I'd missed most about having someone in my life. Even Max had satisfied some of that need to belong, to be comfortable in my own skin, and to be content. It was a lot to ask of anyone, but Jake gave it to me willingly, and I was determined to do my best to return it in kind.

# PINEAPPLE DROP DONUTS

One day I was playing around in the kitchen and found a can of crushed pineapple. Why not include it in a donut? I've been happy with the results, so I thought I'd add it to my stable of donut recipes!

## Ingredients

1 egg, beaten
1 can crushed pineapple (8.5 oz.)
1 cup all purpose flour
1/2 teaspoon baking soda
1/2 teaspoon baking powder
Dash of salt
2 1/2 tablespoons sugar (white)
1/4 teaspoon nutmeg

## Directions

Heat canola oil to 360 degrees while you mix the batter. Put the pineapple in a large mixing bowl, then add the beaten egg and the sugar. Sift the dry ingredients, then add them slowly to the mix. Add the dry ingredients to the wet, and then fold in the extras, until the batter is smooth.

When the ingredients are incorporated, take a teaspoon of batter and rake it into the fryer with another spoon. If the dough doesn't rise soon, gently nudge it with a chopstick, being careful not to splatter oil. After two minutes, check, and then flip, frying for another minute on the other side. These times may vary given too many factors to count, so keep a close eye on the donuts.

Makes around eighteen small donuts.

# Chapter 14

As we approached the house, I saw Momma standing on the porch waiting for us.

"There you are," she said as we joined her. "I'm afraid there's an emergency phone call for Jake."

He frowned and put his hand in his pocket. "Why didn't they call me on my . . . hey, where's my phone?"

She held it up. "It must have fallen out of your pocket when you sat down to eat dinner."

Jake took it from her and said, "Excuse me. I'd better see what this is about." He stepped off the porch, and as he left us, Momma said, "I'm so sorry, Suzanne. I hated to interrupt your date."

"We were just out taking a walk," I said. "It's no big deal."

"Holding hands and walking through the park is a very big deal in most people's minds," she said. "I know it was for your father and me."

"You still miss him, don't you?" I was just beginning to grasp the depth of love my mother had experienced with my father. I knew that was making it harder for her to get on with her life, but it also told me that someone who loved that deeply and completely, someone who was so clearly good at being in love, shouldn't turn her back on it again. If she could find love in her life, why shouldn't she at least try?

"I do miss him, that's a fact. Some days are worse than others, though."

"Wouldn't you like to experience that again, then?"

She looked at me with tears in her eyes. "How could I ever have that again, when most people don't get to experience it even once?"

"There's no limit to the number of times you can fall in love," I said. "And even if there is, shouldn't you be sure before you give up once and for all?"

She was about to answer when Jake rushed up onto the porch. The look on his face told me that his news was not good.

"What happened?" I asked. "Do you have to go?"

"Yes, and you need to come with me."

I felt my heart suddenly drop to my feet.

"Jake, you're scaring me. Did something happen to Grace?"

"It's not Grace," he said. "I'm afraid it's George. He's been in an accident."

"Is he okay?" I kept replaying my friend's last words in my mind. I'd sent him off on an investigation, and something very bad appeared to have happened because of it.

"It doesn't sound like it," Jake said. "He's in the hospital. That's all I know. Before he lost consciousness, he said your name twice, and that he had to talk to you. Grab your jacket and let's go."

I kissed Momma good-bye, and then followed Jake to his car. As we drove to the county hospital, neither of us said a word. I knew I needed to tell Jake what George had told me, but I couldn't bring myself to do it. Finally, just as we entered the parking lot, I knew I didn't have any choice.

"Jake, George was working on something for me connected to Lester Moorefield's murder. I'm the reason he's in there." I looked up at the brick hospital and shuddered. Nearly everyone I had ever known who'd gone in there hadn't made it back out alive. I just hoped that George wasn't going to be added to the list.

"What was he doing?" Jake asked.

"I don't know," I said, fighting back the tears. "He called before you came and said he'd found a new angle that could blow the case open, but when I pressed him for details, he wouldn't say anything except that it was dangerous."

I expected a scolding, but Jake didn't say a word, and I was glad for that.

As we walked into the building, Jake took my hand and finally said, "We can talk about this later, but all that matters right now is George."

We walked to the front desk and Jake said, "We're here to see George Morris."

The woman stationed there checked her computer, and then said, "I'm sorry, but he's not allowed to have visitors."

Jake flashed his badge. "It's important."

She nodded solemnly, and then said, "I understand that, Officer, but he's still in surgery."

"What exactly happened to him?" I blurted out.

"He was in some kind of accident."

"Do you happen to know what kind?" Jake asked.

"It doesn't say. You can wait over there if you'd like, and I'll let you know as soon as I hear anything."

Jake and I took a bench seat by a window.

It looked out onto a tranquil garden, and I wondered how many people had sought solace there over the years for the people they'd just lost.

Jake sat silently for nearly two minutes, and then he jumped up. "Somebody's got to know what's going on around here."

I started to get up when he waved me back down. "Why don't you stay here and wait in case someone comes out to tell us what happened. That way we won't miss anything."

"I hate just sitting here helplessly."

"Suzanne, there's nothing we can do. As soon as I find out anything I'll come back and tell you. If you hear something before I do, call me."

"Okay," I said.

I was still sitting there five minutes later when I heard a familiar voice say, "Suzanne, is something wrong with your mother?"

I looked up to see Penny Parsons, an ER nurse who loved donuts, standing over me. I stood as well. "No, I'm here for George Morris."

She nodded. "I heard he had an accident."

"What exactly happened?"

"He was crossing the street, and someone ran him down. They didn't even stay at the accident scene. If an ambulance hadn't just finished responding to a false alarm in the area, he wouldn't have made it."

"Is it that bad?"

She frowned as she considered her next words. "From what I've heard, it's not good. He was in surgery the last time I checked."

"Could you ask again?"

Penny nodded. "I know you two are close. Hang on a second." She went to the woman at the front, had a brief conversation with her, then tapped a few keys on the computer keyboard. Her face never changed its expression as she read whatever was written there, and I knew at that moment that I'd never play poker with her. I had no idea if the news was good or bad when she walked back to me.

"It's touch and go right now," she said without preamble. "The next forty-eight hours will be critical. At least he's coming out of surgery."

"Can I see him?"

"Suzanne, he wouldn't know you from Betsy Ross right now. He's in rough shape. Give me your cell number, and I'll keep you posted with updates. There's no reason you need to hang around here. Unless I miss my guess, you're going to have to get up in a handful of hours anyway."

"I'll close the shop," I said. I had never done that before, but I didn't know how I'd

261

be able to work with George upstairs fighting for his life.

"You could do that," Penny said, "but it might be a better idea if you kept busy. If you really want to help George, flood the nursing station with donuts." Penny was smiling to show that she was kidding, but I realized it wasn't a bad idea. I knew that the hospital staff was full of professionals who took care of all of their patients as best they could, but if a donut or two or ten dozen would make George's life the slightest bit easier, I'd do it.

"Okay, you've got a deal."

She looked surprised that I'd taken her seriously. "Hey, I was just kidding. Trying to lighten the mood, you know?"

"I know, but you're right. I need to keep busy. Sitting around here is driving me crazy, so I might as well be productive."

Jake spotted me talking to Penny, and he rushed up to us. "Has there been any change in him?"

"She'll bring you up to date," Penny said as she disappeared through a set of nearby doors.

"I couldn't find out anything," Jake said. "Tell me you know something."

I brought him up to speed, and after I was finished, I swear I caught a hint of relief on his face.

"Was there any good news in what I just told you?" I asked him.

"The accident's not related to the murder investigation," Jake said.

"How could you possibly think that? What if George uncovered something that the killer knows would condemn them?"

"That happens in the movies, not in real life," Jake said.

I couldn't believe he was saying that. "You can't be serious."

"Even though it was most likely an accident, you should be careful. Can I give you a ride, or are you going to wait around here?"

"I need to go back home. Penny's going to let me know if there's any change. I'll be getting up early to make donuts."

Jake nodded his approval. "I'm glad you're going to work. You can't do anybody any good sitting around here."

We drove back to my place in near silence, and Jake kissed me briefly before he left.

No matter what he said, I still believed that what had happened to George couldn't have been an accident. Sure, I was still going to make donuts every day, and I planned to flood the hospital with as many as they would take, but that didn't mean I was going to stop investigating.

Momma was waiting up when I got home. "How is he, Suzanne?" She had known George a long time, part of the advantage — and curse — of living in a small town.

"He just got out of surgery. That's all they would tell me. It was a hit-and-run, but I don't know much more than that. I'm going to try to get some sleep so I can make donuts tomorrow."

Momma looked surprised by the news. "Why didn't you stay at the hospital?"

I was ready to snap, not wanting to justify my behavior to her, but then I saw the concerned expression on her face. "A friend of mine is going to keep me updated, and she suggested that if I wanted to make sure George got the best care possible, it might not be a bad idea to bribe the nurses with donuts. Actually, she was just teasing, but if it helps him the least little bit, I'm going to do it."

"What a marvelous idea. If you'd like, I'll deliver the first batch for you."

That's what I loved about my mother. Sometimes, usually when I least expected it, she really stepped up. "Thanks, but I want to do it myself."

She understood. "If you need me, you

know that I'm never more than a telephone call away."

"I know," I said as I kissed the top of her head. "Now I'm going to see about getting a little sleep."

I looked at the clock and saw that it was just past ten. If I was lucky, I was going to get three hours of sleep tonight. I'd made do with less in the past, but never by choice. I could have easily handled it when I was in my twenties, but those days were gone. I had a nap in my future, but not until I took care of business.

The alarm woke me much too soon, and I decided the only way I was going to be able to function at all was to take a cold shower and drink lots and lots of coffee. The second part wouldn't be so hard. I'd given Emma the power to take over our coffee operation at the donut shop, and she'd jumped at the chance with great enthusiasm. No doubt the blend of the day would have enough caffeine to scrape barnacles off a pier, but for once, she wasn't going to hear any complaints from me.

I was ten minutes late getting to the donut shop, and though Emma wasn't due for another twenty, the lights were on in the kitchen when I approached the front door. In the old days I would have barged on in, but after what happened to George, I was on edge. It was worse when I called Emma's number and it went straight to voice mail, a good sign that she was most likely still in bed asleep. I grabbed my phone and dialed 911. "This is Suzanne Hart over at the donut shop. Could you send someone to check things out? I'm out front, so tell them not to shoot me."

My attempt at humor was lost on the night dispatcher. "Don't go into the building until someone from our department arrives."

"That was my plan all along."

Four minutes later, much to my surprise, our chief of police himself showed up. "Chief Martin, you didn't have to come yourself."

"I couldn't sleep, so I was at the station. Hand me your keys."

So much for pleasantries. I did as he asked, and after he silently unlocked the door, he said softly, "Wait here."

"Not a problem."

The police chief drew his gun, and as he pushed the kitchen door open with his free hand, I marveled at how calm he seemed. He was gone thirty seconds, but I swear, I aged three years waiting for the sound of a gunshot.

He came back out, with Emma on his heels.

"Boy, you were serious about my not working any overtime, weren't you? I would have left without a police escort," Emma said.

"What are you doing here? You're never early."

She smiled at me. "I wasn't sure I'd see you today. Dad told me what happened to George, so I decided to come in and make the donuts myself."

"Is your mother here?" She always helped Emma out during those rare times I had to be away.

"No, I decided to wing it myself. How hard could it be? You do it once a week without me. I thought I'd return the favor."

The chief interrupted. "If you two don't need me, I'll be going."

"Thanks for coming so quickly," I said, meaning every word of it. The chief and I had shared a few bad experiences in the past, but it was nice to know that I could still count on him in times of need.

"No need to thank me. It's just part of the job," he said.

After he was gone, I locked the door and turned to Emma. "Should I go, too? It looks like you've got things under control."

She shook her head. "I'd rather you didn't, but if you have to, I'll squeak by. I just wish I could read your handwriting. How many ounces of pumpkin am I supposed to use?"

I followed her back into the kitchen and looked at the recipe. "I wouldn't use any, since these are for applesauce donuts."

She took the recipe from me, peered at it a moment, and then said, "You seriously need to get these on a computer so I can read them."

"Why would I do that? If you can read them without me, you won't need me anymore."

"We both know better than that."

"What happened to your confidence in handling it all by yourself?" I asked.

"I was bluffing," she answered with a big grin. "I'm really glad you're here."

"Let me get a cup of coffee, and we can get started. It smells wonderful, by the way. What is it?"

"You don't want to know, but it tastes heavenly." She paused for a second, and then added, "It might be a little strong, though."

Coming from her, it would probably take rust off a battleship. "That's good. I need something to pep me up."

"Then you're in luck."

I poured myself a cup, and after my first sip, I was afraid my ceramic mug was going to melt before I had a chance to finish it.

But it managed to put a pep in my step. I just wasn't looking forward to crashing later.

As I started mixing, I explained the plan to Emma. She nodded. "So, we're making double batches of everything this morning. Got it."

"Don't say anything about what it's costing us. If we break even today, I'll be a happy camper. We're doing this for George."

"For George," she echoed, and we started getting busy.

By four, we had the first batch of old-fashioned donuts ready, and I had the batter mixed for the second batch. I boxed up our offerings and asked Emma, "Are you sure you're okay with me leaving you?"

"I've got it covered," she said. "Just be sure to come back as soon as you can."

I grinned at her. "You can do it. I have faith in you."

"I'm glad, because that makes one of us."

# CHAPTER 15

The hospital parking lot wasn't exactly empty as I drove up in the darkness, but it was pretty sparse. There was plenty of parking, so I took a space near the front door and grabbed the eight boxes of donuts Emma and I had just made. I wasn't sure how I was going to be able to get the front door open when I saw the large red button for wheelchair access. I hit it, glad that it was there, and walked through the slowly opening doors.

The guard at the front desk looked surprised to see me.

"Can I help you, ma'am?"

"I'm here to see the nurses taking care of George Morris," I said.

"I'm sorry, but you can't go up there." He didn't look like he enjoyed delivering the news, but his sympathy only went so far.

"Has he taken a turn for the worse?"

He glanced at the screen. "I'm sorry, it

doesn't say."

Okay, if that wasn't going to work, maybe I could try another approach. "Could you page Penny Parsons for me?"

He looked at me for a second, and then he smiled and said, "I can't seem to find her number on my call sheet. Maybe a donut would refresh my memory."

I wasn't afraid to use donuts as bribes. I'd learned early on that they could be a wonderful way to grease the wheels. I put the boxes down on his desk, and then flipped open the top one. "I've got chocolate iced, pumpkin, blueberry sprinkles, plain, and double-dipped strawberry."

He looked into the box as though he didn't believe me. "Any glazed?"

"You can catch me on my next run," I said. "These are all old-fashioned."

I started to close the lid when he smiled at me again. "Don't be so hasty. I like old-fashioned, too." He grabbed one of the chocolate-iced donuts and put it on his desk. After a quick call, he said, "She'll be right with you. If you'd like to wait over there I'd be glad to guard these for you."

I smiled at him. "It's not that I don't trust you, but why put temptation in your path? I can handle them myself."

Penny came out frowning, but it disappeared into a grin when she saw me. "I was wondering who would be visiting me this time of morning." Then she spied the donuts. "Suzanne, I feel guilty even joking about that. You didn't have to make those for us."

"It was my pleasure. Any change?"

"No," she said. "We haven't even updated the postings for a while."

"Have you heard how surgery went?"

She lowered her voice. "You didn't hear this from me, but we nearly lost him twice on the table. He's a tough old bird, though, and he pulled through okay. We'll see what happens next."

"Is he awake?"

"They haven't brought him around, and when they do, he's not going to be very helpful. In a way he's lucky. If he'd been hit a few inches either way, he might not be here."

"What's the best-case scenario?" I asked, deeply troubled by the thought of my friend fighting for his life.

"If he gets through the next two days, he'll spend a month recovering. It's pointless to guess right now."

"Will you see that these get properly distributed?" I asked as I tried to hand her the donuts.

"Hang on a second." She turned to the guard. "I need a cart."

"Right away," he said, and a minute later he returned with a black metal cart. I put the donuts down, and then asked him, "Do you want one for the road?"

"I'd better not," he said after some hesitation.

"Go on. We won't tell."

It was all the prodding he needed. He grabbed a double-dipped strawberry donut this time, and thanked me. "These are the best donuts I've ever had in my life."

"Come by Donut Hearts. We're open seven days a week."

As Penny took the cart, I said, "I'll be back in three hours with the glazed donuts. If anything happens between now and then, call me."

"Suzanne, you honestly don't need to bring us any more treats. We'll take care of George. I promise."

"Don't think of it that way. It gives me something to do instead of pacing around the lobby, and if it brightens your lives for a moment or two, then that's even better."

"I understand that you want to do this, but at least wait until tomorrow for the glazed donuts. You don't want to overwhelm them."

"I can do that," I said. I didn't want the influx of donuts to be a curse. "Call me the second you hear something."

"I will."

When I walked back into Donut Hearts, I heard something clatter to the floor. Hurrying back, I found Emma looking as though she were ready to burst into tears. Half a dozen old-fashioned donuts were scattered on the floor.

"Cleanup on aisle four," I said with a smile as I grabbed a broom and dustpan. "Those can be slippery rascals, can't they?"

"How do you manage to do everything at once all by yourself?" she asked me.

"You should have seen the mess I made when I got started in this crazy business. I got distracted the first time I made donuts and forgot to pull a batch out of the fryer. The place smelled like an arson-investigation scene for a week, and I had to throw away the clothes I'd been wearing. This is nothing, trust me."

"I feel a little better, then," she said. "How's George?"

"It's just a matter of wait-and-see now."

Emma nodded. "So far so good, though, right?"

"That's the way we have to look at it. Are

you ready to get started on the yeast donuts now?"

"It's got to be better than this," she said. "You're not going anywhere anytime soon, are you?"

I had to laugh. "Don't worry; I won't take off again until you've got things well in hand."

"Then you might be here for a while."

I patted her shoulder. "You're doing great. Oh, by the way, we aren't doubling the batch of glazed donuts today, after all."

"Didn't they want them?"

"It might be too much of a good thing," I said. "We'll hit them with the glazed tomorrow."

Emma and I cleaned the floor together, and then it was time to make the yeast donuts. The rhythm of the familiar work helped distract me from my dark thoughts, but I still kept waiting for my phone to ring as I worked.

I knew most days that no news was good news, but the silence was driving me crazy. When I hadn't heard anything by three minutes until we were set to open, I decided to call Penny to see if there was any change. When I couldn't get her on the phone, I started to panic.

Emma must have seen it in my expression. "What's wrong, Suzanne?"

"I can't get Penny on the phone."

Emma pointed outside. "Maybe it's because she's out there waiting to get in."

I dropped the phone and raced outside. "Did something happen to George?"

"No, I'm sorry, I didn't mean to alarm you. My shift just ended, so I thought you might like an update in person."

The relief spread through me. "Then he's okay."

"I wouldn't go that far," Penny said, "but at least he's not any worse."

"I've heard better news," I admitted.

"I'm willing to bet that you've heard worse, too. Sorry again for scaring you."

I took a deep breath, and then mustered a smile for her. "And I'm sorry about the way I reacted. It was sweet of you to come by in person. Come on in. Let me buy you a donut and a cup of coffee."

"Thanks, but I'm stuffed from the donuts you brought earlier, and the coffee would keep me awake when I need to sleep. How about a rain check?"

"You've got it."

I was worried about who might update me now that Penny was off shift when she said, "I asked a friend of mine to let you know if there's any change. She's new to

276

the hospital, but she's our kind of people. She'll call if anything happens."

"What's her name?" I asked.

"It's Marsha Nichols."

It didn't take a second for me to smile. "Don't you two get grief hanging around together? I can't imagine there not being jokes about small change."

"Pennies and Nickels kind of go together, don't you think? If we can find staffers named Dime and Quarter, we'll have the full set."

"You might as well smile, right?" I said to Penny. "Thanks for doing this. It means the world to me."

"It's nothing," she said.

"Trust me, I've seen nothing, and this isn't anything close to what it looks like."

After she was gone, I went back inside, flipping the sign to OPEN as I did and turning on the front lights.

Emma was waiting for me by the door. "What did she say?"

"No change," I said, and then realized how that tied in with pennies and nickels. I started laughing, and the hysteria made me continue a little longer than I should have.

"I'm worried about you, Suzanne. Why don't you go home and catch a nap? I can do the heavy lifting around here now that the donuts are all made."

"I'm not that punchy." I explained to her about pennies, nickels, and change, but she still wasn't buying it. "I'll be fine. Trust me."

"You're the boss," she said.

"Good, I'm glad we got that settled. Now, if we only had a few customers, we could start selling donuts." I missed seeing George there, who often came early to have a warm donut and some peace and quiet. Thinking about what had happened to him made me feel sad and guilty all over again, so I decided instead to focus on the task at hand. Since we didn't have any customers yet, I might have time to play with some ideas I'd had for new donuts.

"How are the dishes coming?" I asked Emma as I walked back into the kitchen, making sure to prop the door open so I could see if any customers came in.

"I'm finished, at least until we get some customers."

"Then you take the register, and I'll play with some ideas for new donut flavors we can offer. Care to chime in?"

"No, thanks. I'll leave that up to you."

"I have an idea. You like playing around with the coffees we serve, and I enjoy making new donuts. Some of them are pretty outlandish, I know. Why don't we pick one day a week where we feature something really outrageous, along with our regular offerings, too?"

"We can call it Take a Chance Tuesday," she said, instantly warming to the idea. "If we bundle them as a special, we might get a lot of customers."

"I'm game if you are," I said. "I've got some wild ideas in my Donut Book that I've been too timid to try." I kept a recipe book in back for my old favorites and new ideas, all in the handwriting style that Emma claimed not to be able to read. I knew I should make a copy of it somewhere and store it in a safe place, but I never seemed to get around to it. Life had a habit of getting in the way of my best-laid plans.

Customers started trickling in soon after, and I hadn't made many additions to the book. I hoped later I'd be able to remember what I meant by three-layer donuts and Bismarck madness.

My phone finally rang. "Hello?"

"It's me," Jake said.

"Oh," I replied, trying my best not to sound disappointed.

"I've had warmer greetings from felons I was transporting across the state," he said. "Are we having a problem I don't know about?"

"No, we're good," I said. "I was just hoping the call might be an update about George's condition. You haven't heard anything, have you?"

"That's why I was calling you. You've got some kind of secret network for finding these things out. What's the last you heard?"

"He made it through surgery, so now it's just a matter of wait-and-see," I said.

"That's good news," Jake answered.

"Why don't you swing by and I'll treat you to a donut?"

"You know how cops feel about donut shops," he answered. "There's a natural affinity. I'll try to come, but I can't make any promises. If I don't, save me a couple and I'll get them tonight."

"I'm sorry," I said, "did we have plans?"

"Did I forget to ask you? Suzanne, I'd be delighted to go out with you tonight, if nothing gets in the way between now and then."

"Be still, my heart. You're going to sweep me off my feet with smooth talking like that."

He chuckled, a sound I was growing to love. "You know me. My job is full of conditional promises. If I have to cancel, I'll call you. Otherwise, I'll be by at six."

"Where are we going?"

"That's going to be a surprise," he replied. "Don't worry. It will be fun."

After he hung up, I couldn't help but smile. It was good having Jake in my life, and even my ex-husband was starting to realize that this was real. Max had had his chance with me, and he'd blown it. Moving on with Jake was the best thing I could have done, and according to Momma, I'd taken my own sweet time coming to realize it.

A tall, handsome man with stormy brown eyes and a little too much weight on him came into the donut shop a little after eight, but instead of getting in line behind the other customers, he stood to one side while I waited on everyone there. There was something familiar about him, but that happened to me a lot. When you worked at the front counter of the donut shop, it wasn't all that unusual to run into just about everybody in April Springs at one time or another.

When the line finally faded away, he approached me. "Suzanne Hart?"

That voice was definitely familiar.

"Yes?"

"Nancy told me you wanted to see me."

So, this was her alibi. "Thanks for coming by. You know my name. What's yours?" I asked as I extended my hand.

"A friend of Nancy's," he said, ignoring my hand.

He was going to be a tough customer, obviously. "Let me assure you that I won't share what you tell me with anyone else."

"A donut confessional," he said as a slight smile spread across his face. "Nancy and I were together that night."

"Is there anyone who can verify that, or is there any other way to prove it?" I asked him.

"You don't believe me?"

"I don't know you," I replied, "but even if I did, I would have to have more proof than just your word."

He stared hard at me, then said, "Forget it. I can't help if you're going to be unreasonable." The man leaned in closer toward me and added, "Don't make trouble for me. If my wife hears one word of this, I'll be back for you."

He was gone before I had a chance to even react. There was no doubting the threat he'd just made. How did he expect me to stop other people from talking? I didn't even know his name! Still, I was going to be even more careful until this murder case was resolved. I couldn't afford to duck this man for the rest of my life.

Max came in while I was still contemplating what I'd just heard. "What was Frank doing? Did something happen while he was here? He nearly knocked me over on his way down the street."

"Frank who?" I asked.

"Wheeler. He did just leave here, didn't he?"

"How do you know him, Max?" My ex-husband had a wide array of acquaintances, but I'd never imagined he'd be friends with one of my suspect's alibis.

"We did a play together in Charlotte once. I haven't seen him in years, though. He kind of dropped off the map."

"What sort of man is he?"

Max frowned. "Coming from me, this is probably going to sound odd, but he always had an eye out for his next conquest. No woman in our cast was ever safe from his advances, and not many had the steel to say no to him."

"I imagine he gave you a run for your money, then," I said.

Max shook his head. "No, ma'am. Deep down, that man is cruel. I might not have made the best decisions in my life, but I was never intentionally mean. If I were you, I'd stay out of his way, Suzanne."

"Thanks for the advice. What can I get

you today?"

"Six bear claws," he said.

As I boxed them up, I asked, "Feeling a little peckish, are we?"

"I owe these to someone," he answered as he paid me.

"Even you have to admit, that's a curious debt."

"It's not as interesting as you might think," he said as he collected them and left. Max's words left me a little shaken. He had never been one to be intimidated by anyone, but it was clear that Frank Wheeler had managed to do just that. I was going to add him to my list of suspects. I'd have to ask George . . . For a moment, I'd forgotten my friend was laid up in the hospital fighting for his life. I had grown so used to going to him with questions, but even if I never got another ounce of help from him, I'd still miss him terribly. He was so much more than a customer; he was my friend. I fought the urge to call the hospital and check on him again. Penny had assured me that her friend would let me know the second there was the slightest change in his condition, and I trusted her.

Nine minutes later when my telephone started ringing, I nearly broke it as I flipped it open, hoping against hope that it was good news for a change.

# THE LAST RESORT DONUT

A friend of mine loves these donuts, but I'm not a big fan of them myself. If you're desperate and don't have many supplies on hand, you might want to try these, but trust me, I'd have to be pretty desperate to make them myself. If nothing else, they're pretty easy to make. Consider yourself warned!

## Ingredients
1/2 cup boxed biscuit flour
1/2 cup milk (or water if you don't have milk on hand)
1 tablespoon sugar (white)
1 teaspoon cinnamon

## Directions
Heat canola oil to 360 degrees while you mix the batter. Mix everything together until the batter is smooth.

When the ingredients are incorporated, take a teaspoon of batter and rake it into the fryer with another spoon. If the dough doesn't rise soon, gently nudge it with a chopstick, being careful not to splatter oil. After two minutes, check, and then flip, frying for another minute on the other side. These times may vary given too many factors to count, so keep a close eye on the donuts.

Makes around eighteen small donuts.

# CHAPTER 16

"Hey, Suzanne," Jake said when I answered. "Just touching base again."

"No change so far," I said. "I was just fighting the temptation to call and see if anything's happening myself."

"It's a tough urge to resist, but you have to trust your friends," he said. "Let me know if anything comes up."

"I'll do it," I said. "Where are you?"

"I'm just finishing up in Hudson Creek."

I had to laugh at the thought of Jake interviewing the taciturn builder again. "How's old Vern doing? Is he being any more cooperative than the last time you spoke with him?"

"A part of me wishes he was guilty, but his alibi checks out. I can't bring myself to say that he's innocent of anything."

I couldn't believe what I was hearing. "Jake, did you just tell me I could eliminate one of the suspects on my list?"

He laughed softly. "I could never do that, Suzanne. Officially, I can't sanction your investigation, and it would be wrong of me to help you in any way, and we both know it. Right now I'm just acting as your boyfriend, telling you about my day."

"I appreciate your sharing, more than I can say. Do you want to hear about my day so far?"

"Sure, why not?" he asked.

"I had the most interesting customer today. His name is Frank Wheeler, and he came by to alibi Nancy Patton. When I didn't believe his story, he openly threatened me."

That got a growl from Jake. "What exactly did he say?"

"He warned me that if his wife found out he was cheating on her, he'd be paying me another visit."

"I can be there in twenty-two minutes," Jake said. "In the meantime, I'll have the chief send someone over to keep an eye on you."

"Slow down," I said. "I appreciate the thought, but the threat wasn't immediate. There's no use standing guard outside the donut shop."

That seemed to mollify him a little. "I don't like anybody threatening you."

"I wasn't all that fond of it myself," I admitted. "But what can you do?"

There was a rough edge to his voice as he answered, "More than you might think. Don't worry about this guy. I've got him covered."

"Max was pretty shook up when he ran into him, and he doesn't scare easily."

"Did you bring Max into this, too?"

"He's the one who identified Wheeler for me," I answered. "Max bumped into him as Wheeler was leaving the donut shop."

"Good enough. I am going to have a chat with this Wheeler fellow myself."

"Be my guest," I said. "I don't want him back here any more than you do. Funny, but I could swear I'd seen him before. I just can't put my finger on when."

"Could he be a customer?"

"That's what I thought at first, but I'm beginning to doubt that."

"Don't worry," Jake said. "It will come to you. I'll see you soon."

"Thanks for calling."

"It's my pleasure."

After we were off the phone, I crossed Vern's name off my list. I didn't need to know the specifics of why he was no longer a suspect. If Jake considered him a dead end, I knew that I could, too. That still left a host of people who could have wanted Lester Moorefield dead, but at least I was making some headway, even if it was through the auspices of my boyfriend's investigation.

Just before closing, Emma came out, drying her hands on a dishtowel. "I'm all done in back," she said. "Are we ready to clean up?"

I glanced at the clock. "Eager to get out of here?"

She smiled. "I've got a lunch date, but I can hang around as long as you need me to, Suzanne."

"Is this that same mysterious new man in your life?" My assistant was always falling in love, hard and fast, and she usually crashed that way, too. I watched all of it without an ounce of envy. Having Jake in my life was better than I could have imagined, but it had taken us some time to find each other. I just hoped that Emma had that kind of luck eventually, too.

"Brand spanking new," she said with a smile.

"Come on, give me more than that." The shop was empty, and I'd been toying with the idea of closing myself. Our income still wasn't what it was before Lester's demise, but I'd begun to adjust my output to match it. We could limp along like we were for a while, but I wasn't sure how long we would last on our lowered income. I could make the payments I needed to and cover Emma's salary, but my own pay was on hold until this slump was over. I flipped the sign and locked the door. "I'm not letting you out until you tell me."

She didn't need all that much arm-twisting. "His name is Brian, and he lives in Union Square. We met at the outdoor concert in Hickory last weekend."

"And how would I know young Brian if he walked through that door?"

"By the cuts on his arms and his face, since the door is locked, and he'd have to break in through the glass," she said with a smile.

"So, he's short, heavyset, and has a unibrow. One eye is green, one is brown, and neither one points forward at any given moment. Got it."

"You are so off base," Emma said. "He's a little over six feet tall, lean, with the palest blue eyes I've ever seen in my life."

"Excellent. Just try not to let him break your heart."

"You know me. Risking it all is half the fun," she said.

Had I ever been that young and naïve?

"Go on. You can take off. I can handle what little is left."

"Thanks, boss," she said.

After she was gone, I boxed the last donuts, barely over a dozen, and cleaned the racks and trays. I'd just finished the tables when there was a pecking at the glass.

Grace was there with a slight smile on her face.

As I let her in, I asked, "What are you smiling about?"

"I missed cleanup time today," she said. "I can't believe what happened to George."

"How did you hear?"

"Are you kidding? You know April Springs. It's all over town," she said. "Is he going to be okay?"

"They don't know yet," I answered.

"I'll go see him later." After she spotted the box of donuts on the counter, she asked, "Are those for anyone in particular?"

"Help yourself," I said. "I've got a little coffee left in the pot, but I was about to throw it out. You're welcome to it, if your stomach's feeling particularly stout today."

"Could I pass and have chocolate milk instead?"

"Now you're talking," I said. "I might even join you."

"It's a beautiful day outside," she answered. "As soon as you finish up, we can have ourselves a little picnic."

"I can't think of a reason why not, except for my ever-expanding waistline," I said. "Give me three minutes, and I'll be ready to go."

"I'll look at the paper while you work." Someone had left their copy of the *April Springs Sentinel,* and I'd planned to recycle it. It contained few legitimate news stories, supplemented with lots of advertisements.

I rushed through the last dishes, drained the water, and then rejoined Grace up front, grabbing a pair of milks along the way.

As I approached her, she tapped the paper. "There's something here we should consider."

"Did you find an ad for a new dishwasher for your place?"

"If I did, I'd buy one for you instead," she said. "Mine's still managing to hold on, but I can't believe you do dishes by hand in the sink. It's positively barbaric."

I didn't have the heart to tell her that with my income level at the moment, I could barely afford the soap, let alone a new appliance. "There's never much here at one time. Emma and I manage just fine." It was time to change the subject. "So, what's so fascinating about the *Sentinel*?"

She showed me the paper. It was an editorial about Lester Moorefield's murder, of all things.

I started reading it, and Grace said, "Let's wait until we get outside. If people see us standing in here, they might want some of our donuts."

"Fine," I said with a smile. I turned the lights off as we walked out, and soon we found a bench under a maple that was bursting at its seams with vitality.

"Now may I have that?" I asked, pointing to the paper.

"I'll trade you," she said as she pointed to the box of donuts.

We made the exchange, and I grabbed an apple-filled donut along with the paper. I wasn't happy with it just yet, but if the customers didn't like it, they didn't say. I was constantly trying to improve my recipes, hoping to one day create the perfect donut. So far I'd come close a few times, but never managed to hit the mark. I suppose it gave me something to shoot for.

I started reading Ray Blake's editorial. The man could write; I had to give him that. He'd inherited the paper from his father, but it was probably fading even then. To Ray's credit, he kept hanging on, hoping for better days that I wasn't at all sure would ever come.

"*Murder has come back to our small town, not with guns blasting, but instead perched on butterfly wings. This week, as most of us were safe in our homes with the outside world of danger locked safely away, one of our citizens was taken from us. As more information surfaces about Lester Moorefield, it's difficult to believe that any of us truly knew him. Though his voice filled our businesses, our cars, our homes, none of us realized how much complexity there was to the man behind it. We may never know the entire truth, but it proves one point with no room for doubt. This life can be gone in an instant, and no one knows who will be next.*"

I looked up from the paper, my donut temporarily forgotten. "He knows more than he's written," I said.

"I think so, too. What are the odds Ray will talk to us?"

"We've had our share of run-ins in the past," I said, "but I'm willing to bet he'd be happy to crow about his information. It's clearly not that concrete, or he wouldn't be writing about it on the op-ed page."

"We don't need provable facts," Grace said as she took another bite of her Bavarian cream donut. "Rumors and innuendo are both good, as far as I'm concerned."

I was about to agree when an Irish setter came bounding up, snatching my donut out of my hand before I could make a move to protect it.

"Sim, get back here," I heard a voice cry out. When I looked, I saw that it was one of our suspects, veterinarian and town councilwoman Sherry Lance.

"I'm so sorry," Sherry said as she caught up with her dog. "Sim has been laid up, and he's feeling a little rambunctious just now. I'll gladly pay for that donut I just saw him swallow whole."

"It's fine," I said. "I have more. You're welcome to join us."

As she slipped the collar back over her dog's neck, she said, "No, thanks."

"You say that like they're poison," I said, suddenly tired of having my offerings disparaged. "One's not going to hurt anyone." Unless it's Lester, but that really hadn't killed him anyway.

"One leads to two, two leads to six, and that leads me back to where I refuse to go again."

"Point taken," I said. "I promise to never offer you a donut again."

She looked at me a second, and I could swear I saw tears in her eyes. "I love donuts. Believe me."

"It's kind of hard to, the way you've been acting."

Sherry nodded. "I'm sure it is. Suzanne, I'm not from around here, so you'd have no way of knowing it, but I was a heavy kid, and I mean heavy. Donuts were my thing, and I could eat them all day long if I had enough money in my pocket. When I went away to college, I swore I'd change myself. I started exercising, cut out most of the things I loved to eat, and transformed myself into someone no one I'd grown up with even recognized. Since then, it's been a constant battle for me. I know if I slip just once, it's all going to be over for me, and I refuse to go back to being that heavy girl."

I dusted off my hands. "I apologize. I had no idea."

She grinned at me. "Why do you think I moved so far from home as soon as I graduated? No one knows why, and that's the way I'd like to keep it."

"Your secret is safe with us," I said. "Right, Grace?"

"I swear," she said as she crossed her heart.

Sherry smiled at us both. "To be honest with you, it feels kind of good getting that off my chest."

"We're here anytime," I said, "and if you

don't want to risk temptation coming by the donut shop, you could always call me at home any time before seven."

She laughed. "You keep odd hours, don't you?"

"You don't know the half of it," Grace said. "How she found a boyfriend willing to put up with that I'll never know."

"Some of us are just lucky, I guess," I said.

Sherry looked uncomfortable with the turn our conversation had just taken, but I couldn't imagine why. "Is there anyone special in your life at the moment?" I asked her.

"There was," she admitted, "but he turned out to be a rat. No, that's not fair; I've treated pet rats that were the sweetest things. Scoundrel fits him better."

"Anyone we know?" Grace asked.

I never would have asked that particular question, and I certainly never dreamed that she'd answer it, but we must have caught her in a moment of weakness. "It's Cam," she said so softly I wasn't sure I heard it right.

"Cam Hamilton?" I asked. "What did he do?"

"He stood me up one too many times," she said. "I'll never forget the last time I took that from him. As a matter of fact, it was the night Lester Moorefield was murdered. He and Cam never did get along. I'm sure Cam wishes he'd been with me now. I could have given him an alibi, if anyone asked him for one. I was at a diner in Hudson waiting half the night for him. The waitress can vouch for me, but Cam's on his own. Good riddance," she said. "I'm better off without him."

"I don't doubt that you are," Grace said.

"Where exactly were you waiting?" I asked.

"I don't want to talk about it," she answered.

"It could help," I suggested. I had a feeling that Sherry was about to answer when her cell phone rang.

After a hurried conversation, she said, "Sorry, but I've got to go. It's part of the joy of being a vet."

After she left, with Sim firmly in tow, I asked Grace, "Was it just me, or was that alibi just a little too convenient?"

"It did seem planned. It was almost as though she wanted us to ask her about it. I wonder why she wouldn't tell us the name of the diner? Maybe she didn't want us to check it out."

"Do you believe her?" I asked.

"I'm not sure. How about you?"

"If she's telling the truth, Jake could track it down in a heartbeat. Who knows? Maybe he already has."

"What, you two don't share crime-busting tips on your dates?" Grace asked.

I nodded. "As a matter of fact, he just told me that Vern Yancey's alibi holds up."

She looked at me as if she didn't believe me. "You're kidding, right?"

"No, ma'am. He actually opened up and shared."

"Sweet. Go ahead and sic him on Sherry."

"Why don't we hold off on that for now? I don't want to go to the well too often with him. He might shut me out completely."

"It's a fine line you're dancing," Grace admitted as she opened the donut box back up. After thirty seconds of consideration, she closed it back without taking a donut.

"Getting full?" I asked.

"Me? Not likely. That's all I want of these, though. No offense."

"Trust me, there are days I can't stand the sight of them. Thank goodness they aren't all that frequent. We can toss these out and go find Ray."

"Hang on," she said as she grabbed my arm before I could toss the donut box into a nearby bin. "There's no need to be so dramatic. I might want one later."

"You don't have to on my account," I said. "I really do understand."

"Suzanne, don't make me get tough with you. Now hand over the donut box and nobody has to get hurt."

I did as she asked, and smiled. "I'm glad you're my friend."

"That's handy, because I'm not going anywhere."

Grace stopped to put the donuts in the backseat of her car, and we made our way over to the newspaper office. It was time to speak with Ray and find out how much he knew about Lester Moorefield's murder, and what he speculated had happened to the man. Hopefully it would allow us to eliminate another suspect or two and make things just a little more manageable.

When we got there, we found a note on the door of the newspaper office.

*"Gone to a fire. Back when it's out."*

I looked around and smelled the air. "Do you smell smoke?"

Grace tried as well, but then shook her head. "Maybe it's somewhere else."

"Or it might not be that kind of fire."

"What do we do in the meantime?" she asked me.

"We could always wait," I said.

"I'm not particularly good at doing that.

We could get in my car and drive around until we come up with a better idea."

"Fine," I said. Before we left, I asked, "Do you have a piece of paper and a pencil on you?"

"Will a pen do?" she asked as she handed both items to me.

"That will be great." I scrawled a note.

*"Ray, came to ask you some questions. There could be a story angle in it for you. Eight is too late, so call before that. Suzanne Hart."*

Grace had been reading over my shoulder. "That should get his attention."

"Did I tease him too much with it?"

She shook her head. "I think it's exactly the right amount. Let's go."

We were back to her car when my cell phone rang. Was it Jake, or maybe an update from the hospital?

I couldn't wait to answer it either way.

# CHAPTER 17

"What's this story idea you're pitching, Suzanne?" Ray asked the second I said hello. "Did something happen to George Morris? I just left the hospital and there wasn't any change in his condition."

"I haven't heard anything new about him, either," I said. "Do you have a minute?"

"I'm in my office, so if you can get here in five minutes, I can give you twenty if you need it."

"We'll be right there," I said, and started to hang up.

"Hold on. Who is included in this 'we'? Is Jake Bishop with you? I've been hounding him for a quote all day, and all he'll say is 'no comment.'"

"No, it's Grace Gauge," I said.

"Okay, I'll talk to her, too," he said.

"We'll be right there."

We found a spot in front of the newspaper office, and Ray answered on the first knock.

"Come in," he said as he looked up and down the street.

"Who are you looking for?" I asked.

"You can never be too cautious," he said.

"Paranoid much?" Grace asked softly, but Ray must have caught it.

"Someone's been following me around; I can feel it. I just haven't been able to spot them yet. Don't worry, though, I will."

Once he was safely behind his desk, Ray started to open up. "The note you left was cryptic, Suzanne. Did you do that on purpose?"

"I wanted to get your attention," I admitted.

"Well, it worked. What do you have for me?"

"I hate to admit it, but right now, I've got more questions than answers," I said.

His face clouded a little. "I thought you said there was a story angle in it for me. You didn't lie, did you?"

"If we get the right answers, we'll let you know what we come up with," I said, hoping that I wasn't promising too much.

"Sorry, but that's the best we can do right now," Grace added.

It seemed to work, though.

"Fire away," he said as he leaned back.

"What do you know about Lester Moorefield's murder that you're not writing about in the paper?" I asked. That was an easy first question, and it could open the floodgates if Ray felt like sharing what he'd been able to find out.

"More than you or your boyfriend know," Ray said.

For some reason, he was on the defensive. Maybe sharing didn't come easily for him. "I'm here asking for your help. You're sitting on something you think might be big. Do I have to even mention that George felt the same way, and decided not to share his information with me? You don't want something to happen to you, too, do you?"

At least that made him think.

"You've got a point. What I'm going to say here is in confidence, however. If you repeat it, or attribute it to me in any way, shape, or form, I'll call you both liars to your faces. Do we understand each other?"

"Perfectly," I said, and Grace nodded in agreement, as well.

"Good. Here's what I've got so far. Lacy Newman looks to be my number one suspect. I can't prove it, but I believe she killed Lester."

"I don't get why she's even a suspect," I said.

"Are you kidding me? She'd do anything

to protect her husband's memory. Arthur Newman killed himself. You knew that, didn't you?"

"I heard it was heart failure," Grace said.

Ray shrugged. "Isn't that what kills all of us, after all? It's a pretty sweeping cause of death, and this time, it covered up a suicide. From what I've heard, he overdosed on sleeping pills when he heard there was going to be an investigation into his accounts at the bank, and he couldn't face the disgrace. Old Doc Mooney signed the death certificate the way he did out of respect for Lacy."

"We can't exactly ask him, can we?" I asked, since Mooney had died years ago.

"No, but I found his nurse living in Sarasota. She wouldn't testify to it, but she said there was something odd about the way the whole thing was handled."

"But why does it matter, after all these years?" Grace asked.

"Think about it," I said. "Lacy's memory of her husband is all she's got left of him, besides that garden they grew together."

"She wouldn't kill anyone just to keep a secret," Grace said firmly.

Ray rubbed a hand through his thinning hair. "You'd be surprised how powerful that can be as motivation."

"Who else have you been looking at?" I asked.

"Isn't there anything you can give me?" he asked.

He had a point. I had to give him something. "We've got folks from all walks of life, and our suspect list is pretty broad right now. I'd give you more, but I don't want to accuse anyone of anything until I've got more evidence."

"But when you do, you'll share with me, right?"

"You can count on it."

Ray nodded. "I suppose that's all I can ask. The other suspect I have is pretty powerful around here."

He was actually trying to tease me with something I already knew.

"Cam Hamilton," I said.

Ray looked startled by the name. "Where did you get that?"

"We spoke with Cara Lassiter. She gave us a list of people Lester went after, and our mayor was pretty high on the list. When we spoke with him about it, he was dismissive, and then he got a little defensive when we pursued it further."

"Wouldn't that reaction make sense if he were innocent?" Grace asked.

"Somebody killed Lester Moorefield," I said.

"I personally think his wife did it," Grace said.

That got Ray's attention. "He was married?"

"To a woman in Union Square," I said.

Ray grabbed a pencil. "That's more like it. What's her name?"

Grace was about to tell him when I said, "Not yet. You'll get her name later."

"I deserve at least that much now," he said.

I wasn't excited about turning one of our suspects over to Ray, but he had been forthcoming with us. What could it hurt? "I'll tell you. In twenty-four hours." That should give us time to speak with her again before we loosed the press on the woman.

"Make it twelve and we've got a deal," Ray said.

"Keep pushing, and it will be forty-eight," Grace said, getting into the spirit of the negotiation.

"Okay, okay, it's one full day."

"Do you have anything else?" I asked him.

Ray scanned a list in front of him. "No one like Lacy and Cam. Then again, I didn't know Lester was married. Let's see, I've been looking at Sherry Lance and Cara, too.

Can you imagine having to work with that man every day?"

I wasn't about to tell him that we'd eliminated Sherry from our list.

Before I could respond, Grace said, "It's not much of a motive for murder. How hard is it to get another job?"

"As a matter of fact, Cara already found a new program there to produce," I said. "Is that all you have?"

"Come on, I think that's a lot."

"It is," I said as Grace and I started to leave.

"Don't forget your promise," Ray called out.

"Which one?"

"Both of them. You're going to give me Lester's wife tomorrow, and then when you figure it out, I get the scoop."

Out on the sidewalk, I looked at Grace. "Are you thinking what I'm thinking?"

"What, that a cheeseburger from the Boxcar would be great about now?"

I laughed at my friend. "We'll pick up a bite on the way to Union Square. We need to see if we can wring anything more out of Nancy Patton before we give her name to Ray."

"You're right. There's not much chance she'll talk to us after we do that," Grace answered.

We grabbed sandwiches at a place along the way that couldn't touch Trisha's fare at the Boxcar, but it was quick, and not too pricey. When we got to Nancy's shop, I wasn't sure at first that she was even there. The bell over the door that announced us didn't stir up any signs of life.

"Hello?" Grace called out.

"Shh," I said. "Let's see if we can surprise her."

We walked through the shop to the back room, and I was surprised to hear the sound of someone crying.

"Nancy?" I asked softly as I tapped on the doorjamb. "Are you all right?"

She dabbed at her eyes with an antique lace handkerchief. "I didn't hear you come in. I'm sorry."

"We didn't mean to interrupt," I said. "What happened?"

"Men," she said, and then began to cry again.

Grace moved past me and touched her shoulder lightly. "They can be real prizes, can't they?"

"I know there are good ones out there," Nancy said, "but I never seem able to find any of them."

"Are you talking about Lester?" I asked gently.

"What?" She looked startled by the suggestion. "No, we were finished a long time ago. The only reason he wanted to stay married was so he could use it as an excuse if someone got too close to him. I didn't mind, it wasn't inconveniencing me in any way. At least not until Frank came into the picture."

"Your alibi," I said.

"He's more than that," Nancy admitted. "I thought we were in love, but that was before I knew that he was digging into my life."

"What do you mean?"

"I just found out he thinks I killed Lester!" she said, and then started crying again.

After she composed herself, I asked, "Did he actually accuse you of it?"

She shook her head. "Not in so many words, but he might as well have. He's been going around April Springs in disguise trying to find out what really happened."

I knew I'd seen the man before, and something finally clicked. "He was dressed as a clown, wasn't he?"

"How could you possibly have known that? It's Frank's favorite disguise."

"I threw him out of the donut shop," I

admitted.

"Good for you. I wish I'd had the nerve to throw him out of my life."

"Don't be so hard on yourself," Grace said. "It happens."

"Too often to me," she said. "None of this would have happened if Frank hadn't asked me to marry him. The worst part of it is, he has to know I didn't do it. He was proposing to me about the time someone killed Lester, but he won't listen to reason." She dabbed at her eyes. "I think he's using the murder as an excuse to back out of it, especially now that I'm free to marry him."

"It sounds as though you're better off without him," Grace said.

"I don't know. Maybe you're right, but it's too soon to tell. It doesn't matter. He's gone. He didn't even have the nerve to tell me to my face. All I got was a note."

She pointed to a crumpled note on her desk that appeared too brief to be a good-bye.

"I'm sorry," I finally said, when I could think of nothing else to say.

As we left, Grace said, "I feel bad about turning her over to Ray. She deserves better from us, don't you think?"

"If she's telling the truth," I said as I got out my cell phone.

313

Grace put a hand on mine to stop me from dialing. "What do you mean?"

"It seems awfully convenient that her alibi left town so suddenly. All we have is her word that she didn't kill her husband."

"Is that why you're calling Jake?"

I looked at her, startled by the idea. "I'm letting Ray know her name early. He might be able to get something else out of her."

"We weren't going to tell him until tomorrow."

"What can I say? Plans change." I dialed Ray's number and gave him Nancy's name and location, told him about Frank Wheeler, too, and the newspaper publisher promised to be in Union Square in half an hour.

Grace was frowning at me when I hung up.

I took a deep breath, and then said, "I'm sorry you don't approve."

"I'm just surprised, that's all."

"Grace, this is murder we're talking about here. If she killed her husband, it has to come out. Ray is better than you think. He might get something out of her that we couldn't manage to."

"And if he can't?" she asked.

"Then she gets her tears out of the way in one day, instead of stretching it out into two. It's the best we can do. I need for things to be resolved, and sooner rather than later."

"You're fighting for your business," Grace said. "I can understand that."

"It's more important than that. I need to protect my reputation. I haven't said anything to you about it, but Lester's murder is slowly killing my business."

"Is it really that bad?"

"Enough people have stopped coming in to turn my black ink red, and I don't have that much in reserve. The pot has to be stirred, whether we like what that leads to or not."

Grace seemed to think about that, and then nodded. "You're right. I don't know what's gotten into me. I must be getting soft."

"Lacy's involvement can't be easy on you," I said.

"It shouldn't matter, if she's the killer. Who's next on our list?"

"I want to go to the hospital and check on George," I said. "I can't believe we haven't heard anything new."

Grace glanced at her watch. "Okay. I should have time."

"Is there somewhere you need to be?"

She admitted, "I've got a conference call with my boss, but I could probably put it off until tomorrow."

"Are you crazy? Your job has to come first. I can drop you off on the way to the hospital."

As I started driving back, she said, "I hate to feel like I'm bailing out on you, Suzanne."

I smiled at her briefly. "Are you kidding me? You're the most supportive person I've ever known in my life."

"I'm telling your mother that you said that," Grace answered with a grin of her own.

"Go ahead. I'll just deny it."

"You would, wouldn't you?"

Our conversation was interrupted by my cell phone. Was this the news I'd been waiting for?

It was almost as good. After I found out who it was, I said, "Hi, Jake."

"Hello, sunshine. How are you?"

"Pretty good. How about you?"

"I'm okay. I'm just running a little behind again," he said.

"Care to tell me why?" It was worth asking the question.

"I would if I could," he said, and then hung up.

"What was that all about?" Grace asked me.

"I'd tell you if I had the slightest clue," I admitted.

I dropped Grace off at her car, and then started toward the hospital. As I drove, I noticed that Cara Lassiter was walking in that direction. I pulled over and honked my horn, but she didn't look at me.

"Cara, it's Suzanne," I said.

She turned then, and smiled at me. "I thought you were another hound trying to get my attention. What's happening to our quaint little town?"

"I suppose there are wolves everywhere," I answered. "Can I give you a ride somewhere?"

"That would be great," she said.

After she got into my Jeep, I asked, "Where are you heading?"

"I'm on my way home. My blasted car died on me again, and I can't afford to get it fixed just yet. When my big check comes, I'm going to trade it in on something that runs."

"Who's sending you money?" I asked.

She lowered her voice, though it was just the two of us in the car. "I'm not telling anyone yet, but I recently won a bit of money in the lottery."

"You mean people actually make money playing?" I asked.

"I know, it's crazy how the odds are, but every now and then I put five dollars down, just in case. This time I won. It's not a fortune, but it should make my life easier. Suzanne, I'd appreciate it if you didn't spread that around."

"I won't tell a soul. Congratulations."

"Thanks. Where are you headed?"

"I'm going to the hospital to see George Morris," I said.

"I forgot you two were friends. Any word on his condition? The last I heard, he was still unconscious."

"That's why I'm going. He's been out a long time."

"You can let me off right here," she said as she motioned to a nearby intersection. "I can walk the rest of the way."

I pulled over, and she hopped out. "Thanks again."

"I expect a ride in that new car of yours," I said.

"You've got a deal."

I had a hard time believing that Cara could be a killer, but it couldn't be harder than Grace believing that about Lacy. It was difficult not to let the fact that I liked someone cloud my judgment. I didn't know how Chief Martin did it, and I began to have a little sympathy for him, unusual for me.

I couldn't get in to see George, a fact I learned when I checked in at the intensive care unit. Was Penny on duty? I asked a nurse, and was told to wait, which I had never been any good at.

Penny came out ten minutes later. "Hey, Suzanne. You didn't bring any more donuts, did you? There are still some in the nurse's lounge."

"I'll bring fresh donuts in tomorrow morning," I said. "Any news on George?"

"He's still unconscious," she admitted, and I could have sworn she looked worried about it.

"It's not good, is it?" It broke my heart to say those words.

"I told you before, there's no way we can tell, but if he's not alert by morning, we might have something to worry about."

"I know you can't tell me anything officially, but surely you've got an opinion. I'm a big girl. I can take it."

"I don't believe in speculating," she said firmly. "I've been wrong too many times in the past."

She had just finished speaking when a code for the ICU section was called over the intercom.

Without a word, Penny sprinted back, and I was left to wonder if George was going to make it, or if he was taking his last breath as I stood helplessly by.

# A Twist On Textured Donuts

This is a recipe I borrowed from a friend of mine. They're a nice change of pace from standard donuts, and they have the added benefit of being simple to make and not requiring many ingredients. We like them for dipping into tasty additions like apple butter, strawberry jam, and even melted chocolate!

## Ingredients

1 cup all purpose flour
1 teaspoon baking powder
1/4 teaspoon salt
1 cup buttermilk (2% or whole milk will also do, even water in a pinch)

## Directions

Heat canola oil to 360 degrees while you mix the batter. When it's blended well, you're ready to go! Take a teaspoon of batter and rake it into the fryer with another spoon. If the dough doesn't rise soon, gently nudge it with a chopstick, being careful not to splatter oil. After two minutes, check, and then flip, frying for another minute on the other side. These times may vary given too many factors to count, so keep a close eye on the donuts.

Makes around eighteen small donuts.

# CHAPTER 18

Fifteen minutes later Penny walked back out, her face a mask of sadness. The news I'd been dreading appeared to be at hand.

"He didn't make it, did he?" I asked as she approached.

She just shook her head, and I felt myself start to collapse. Penny managed to break my fall and steer me to a chair. "It's not George. It's not George."

It took a few seconds for the words to sink it.

"We just lost Mr. Hickman," she said. "Nobody expected him to pull through, but it's never easy losing one of your favorites."

"What about George?"

"Still no change," she said.

"That's good news, right?"

"It's not bad," Penny said.

"Are you going to be working much longer?"

"I'm at the start of my shift. I'll call you if

there's any change, I promise."

I nodded. "I don't know how you do it."

"We lose too many in the ICU, but we save some, too. That's what I have to keep focusing on. I'll see you later, Suzanne."

"Bye," I said as she headed back inside. There were times I fussed about having to make donuts seven days a week to keep my business afloat, but it was never a matter of life and death. I didn't know how the doctors and nurses managed to deal with it, but I was really glad that someone could.

I decided to stop by the donut shop on the way home and check on my flour order. It had been delayed two weeks before, and I was running low. I'd forgotten to call the supplier when Grace had shown up today, and if I wanted to keep making donuts, I had to have flour on hand to do it.

After I got that straightened out, I was locking the shop up when I noticed Gabby watching me from next door. I almost ignored her, since it had been a long day, but that would just be delaying the inevitable. Taking a deep breath, I walked over to her shop, and was surprised when she came out to meet me.

"I dated Lester Moorefield," she said in a rush. "I didn't know he was married or I would have never gone out with him in the first place." She looked relieved to finally tell someone.

"When did you break it off?" I asked.

"Six months ago. He wouldn't let me tell anyone we were going out, and I got tired of all the secrecy. I dropped him, but I didn't kill him, Suzanne."

Six months was a long time for someone to hold a grudge, even Gabby. "I believe you," I said.

She looked into my eyes. "You really do, don't you?"

"Yes, ma'am."

Gabby asked, "Should I tell Chief Martin about it?"

"I don't see why you would," I said. "I wouldn't deny it if he asked you, but I don't think it's something anyone needs to know but us, do you?"

Gabby nodded. "Yes, that's excellent advice. Thank you, Suzanne."

"You're welcome," I answered. I couldn't see Lester and Gabby together, not that I wanted to picture that particular pairing in my mind, and I didn't think it was anybody's business but hers. As I drove home, I marveled yet again at how anyone could keep a secret in April Springs. For such a small town, it was a very busy place, particularly behind the scenes and away from

Springs Drive.

"Cam, what are you doing here?" I'd seen a strange car parked in our driveway, but I'd assumed it belonged to someone my mother knew. Our mayor was sitting on the steps, lying in wait for me.

"We need to talk," he said. The jovial mayor was gone, replaced by a man who looked as though he meant business.

"What about? I'm expecting Jake Bishop any second. You've met the state police inspector, haven't you?"

"Our paths have crossed," he said as he stood. "I'll make this quick, then. Sherry lied to you."

"About the affair?"

"Her alibi. I was at my place waiting for her that night, and she's the one who didn't show up. I don't know why you keep digging into this. You're going to make a killer have reason to come after you if you don't stop."

"Is that a threat?"

"I told you before, I don't make threats. You're playing with something dangerous here, and you can't count on your boyfriend to keep you safe."

He started down the steps as I asked, "How did you know that I even talked to

Sherry?"

"She told me," Cam said. "I guess if she says it enough, she'll start to believe that it's true. The woman's setting you up, Suzanne."

"And I should believe you?" I asked.

"It's the truth. You know what? On second thought, I don't care what you do. Just quit butting into my life."

"Watch your tone of voice, young man," my mother said from behind me. I hadn't even heard her open the door.

Cam turned and smiled at her. "Good evening, Dorothy."

"Don't even think about it," Momma said.

"What's that?"

"Trying that smooth line on me. I heard what you just said, and how you said it. You must be growing tired of being our mayor."

He laughed at that. "Why do you say that?"

"By the way you're acting, it might be time for a change."

That brought out a snort. "Who's going to beat me in the next election, you?"

"I have more friends than you might realize," she said.

"Momma, it's okay. I've got this."

She gave me a quick look of dismissal, and then turned back to the mayor. "You may leave now."

"I'm not afraid of you, Dorothy."

"It's 'Mrs. Hart' to you," she said, icing him with her best glare.

He left then, but I could tell the Hart ladies were not his favorites in the world. Once his car was gone, Momma turned to me. "What did he say to you?"

"He keeps threatening me, telling me to butt out, but then he claims it wasn't a threat at all."

"The man's got sharp teeth," she said.

"Are you telling me I should stop nosing around?" Momma had expressed her unhappiness with my investigations in the past, and I was certain this wasn't going to be any different. I understood her desire to protect me, no matter how old I was, but that didn't mean I had to like it.

My mother shook her head as she said, "On the contrary. What can I do to help?"

I couldn't believe what I was hearing. "Are you serious?"

"I don't joke about things like this," she said. "Cam Hamilton has won his last election if I have anything to say about it."

"Just because of the way he treated me?"

Momma shook her head. "I've heard rumors about him in the past, but I've never given them much credence. Seeing how he just treated you has changed my mind. The man's a bully at heart, and that's something I will not tolerate."

Suddenly I felt sorry for our mayor. My mother had locked him in her sights, and I knew there was no way she was going to give up until he was thrown out of office.

"I repeat," she said. "What can I do?"

"I need to confirm Sherry Lance's alibi. She claims she was at a restaurant waiting for Cam the night of the murder, but she won't tell me where she was."

"Give me a moment."

I followed her inside, and Momma went straight to the telephone. I heard her say Sherry's name, ask the question I had, and she waited for an answer. After a moment, she thanked her and hung up. "She was at the East Side Diner in Bonham's Landing. An older woman named Betty waited on her all night."

As Momma looked up the number for the restaurant, I asked, "Why would she tell you, when she wouldn't say a word to me?"

"Unlike our mayor, Sherry understands the power structure around here. Hmm. Should we run her for mayor against Cam?"

"They were dating until just recently," I said.

"That could certainly make for an interesting matchup," she said as she dialed the number. "Hello," she said when she got them on the line. "I need to speak with one of your waitstaff. Her name is Betty." There was a pause, and then Momma said, "I need one minute of her time. If I have to come down there, it will be considerably more inconvenient for you."

After a second, Momma asked, "Betty? I need to ask you about a woman named Sherry Lance. She was in there this week. Yes. Describe her, please. What night was this? Thank you for your time."

Momma hung up and smiled at me. "She remembers Sherry, all right. It was the night of Lester's murder, too."

"That was brilliant getting her to describe Sherry. I wouldn't have thought of doing that myself."

"I'm willing to bet that you would," Momma said. "After all, you got your skills from your mother."

"So, I can cross Sherry's name off my list of suspects."

"But Cam Hamilton's stays on."

"Are you kidding? I'm ready to highlight it in yellow," I answered.

"Who else is on your slate of suspects? Perhaps I can help with one of those, as well."

I was about to take her up on it when I smelled something in the kitchen. "Is something burning?"

"The gravy," she said as she rushed into the kitchen. I followed her, and the pan on the stovetop was smoking. Momma grabbed the pan and poured it into the sink. "I'm afraid that's ruined."

"We'll just have to do without the gravy."

"I'm so sorry that I forgot to tell you. Jake is coming by to take me out tonight."

She smiled brightly. "Then we don't need gravy, do we?"

I looked around and saw that she had just pulled her famous lemon chicken out of the oven. "You cooked for nothing."

"Don't believe that for a second. We can have chicken salad, chicken wraps, and chicken baked potatoes this week."

"You know I love chicken," I said with a grin.

"When is he picking you up?"

I glanced at my watch. "I've got ten minutes to make myself beautiful."

"You'll need considerably more than that," she said.

"Thanks for the vote of confidence," I said as I started for the stairs.

"Don't be that way. All I meant to say was that you have your work cut out for you.

Can I help?"

"No, I think you've done enough."

"Excellent," she said, missing my sarcasm completely.

I had to laugh as I took the stairs two at time. It was a nice change of pace having Momma on my side. She had pull in April Springs that I would never have. If I were Cam Hamilton, I'd be scared stiff at the moment. He'd better not plan on redecorating his office; I doubted he'd be keeping it much longer. As I showered, I thought about who was left on my list of suspects now that Sherry was out. Cam was at the head of it, followed by less likely suspects like Lacy, Cara, Nancy, and Frank Wheeler. Then again, it could be someone who hadn't shown up on my radar yet. If Jake could solve this case, or even Chief Martin, I wouldn't mind in the least. Whatever it took to get me out from under being suspected of murder was fine with me, and I'd gladly give someone else the credit.

I was ready a full thirty seconds before Jake was due to arrive, so I walked out on the porch to greet him when he drove up. When my cell phone rang two minutes later, I groaned a little when I saw who was calling. I wasn't in the mood to talk to the man on the other end of the line, but I couldn't afford to let it go to voice mail, either.

"It's Ray Blake. Am I interrupting something?"

"Not at the moment," I said. "What's going on?"

"I just confirmed Nancy Patton's alibi, and Frank Wheeler's, too."

"That was quick work," I said.

"It's a good skill for a newspaperman to have."

"How did you do it?"

"I found Frank in a bar in Hudson Creek, and as long as I kept buying drinks, he was willing to keep talking. The man's bitter. He thought he was in love with Nancy, and then he found out she was married. He told me he proposed, but when he found out about Lester, he didn't want to marry a woman who was that good at keeping secrets."

"He confirmed the timing of the proposal?"

"In great detail. He even showed me the empty ring box. He said it was his good-luck talisman now, and he wants it as a reminder of how close he came to marrying Nancy."

"He sounds like a real prize," I said.

"He just got caught up in the moment," Ray said. "Anyway, I promised I'd let you know what I found out."

"Thanks, Ray," I said as I hung up. I'd marked them off my list in my mind with a pencil, but I changed that to ink now. I couldn't wait to tell Jake. Only where could he be?

I was about to give up on him when he drove up.

As he got out of his car, he handed me a bouquet of daisies and said, "Suzanne, I'm sorry I'm late."

I took the flowers from him. "You're forgiven. It's nice that you remembered daisies were my favorite."

"Are they?" he asked with a grin. "I just saw these at the side of the road and dug them up." His joke was obvious, since they were clean, pristine, and wrapped in green florist paper.

"Then you get points for being resourceful. Where are we going?"

"I thought we'd eat here," he said.

"Sorry, you just lost all the points you got for bringing me flowers. You promised me a meal out."

"Don't be so quick to take my points away," he said as he reached toward the backseat of his car. There was a blanket there, along with a picnic basket. "I thought we could eat in the park together. Is that okay?"

"It sounds great. I know just the spot."

We walked over to my thinking tree, and I took the blanket from Jake and spread it out on the grass. Dusk was fast approaching, and there was the slightest chill in the air, something that I loved this time of year.

"What did you get?" I asked as I reached for the basket.

"Hang on a second. I'll serve you," he said.

I took a seat, and Jake opened the basket. He looked inside, then did a double take. "That's not right," he said.

"What is it?"

Jake started pulling things out of the basket. Once he had emptied it out, there were four containers of baked beans and a jug of lemonade. And that was all. The drink had a Shrewsberry label on it, which explained everything. Shrews, as we liked to call the restaurant in Union Square, had never gotten an order right in their life. We'd long ago stopped going there, but evidently Jake wasn't aware of their tendency to get things wrong.

"Wow, you sure know all of my favorites," I said with a grin.

"This is supposed to be fried chicken, potato salad, and sweet tea."

"Did you order the beans?"

Jake nodded. "Yes, but not this much."

"Hold on. I'll be right back."

I walked over to the house and found that Momma had just taken the foil off her chicken. "Any chance I could hijack that?" I asked.

"What happened to Jake?"

"He brought over a picnic basket full of baked beans."

"They weren't even in a container?" My mother looked suitably horrified.

"Oh, yes, but that's all the restaurant packed for him."

"He must have gotten them from Shrewsberry's."

I laughed. "You should have seen his face. Care to join us? There's plenty of baked beans, and it's only fair, since you're contributing the chicken."

"No, you two have fun. Don't let it spoil the moment for you."

I grinned at her. "Are you kidding? Just think what a great story this will make later."

I grabbed a sweater, and then returned with the chicken to find that Jake had one of the baked beans containers open and was eating them with a spoon. "You know what? These are pretty good."

"I'm glad you like them. You certainly got

enough of them." I presented the chicken to him, and we had a good laugh about it all. That was one of the things I cherished about Jake. We could make the best of just about any situation, while life with Max had always been a little work.

After we ate and cleaned up our trash, Jake said, "You were pretty specific about where we should put the blanket. Why this spot in particular?"

"Look up," I said, and pointed to the sky.

Jake whistled softly under his breath. "The stars are beautiful."

"And there's not a light in view to break up the sight," I said. We lay back on the blanket looking up at the sky and holding hands. At some point I must have fallen asleep, because I felt Jake gently rocking my shoulder.

"Hey," he said. "I know I'm not Mr. Excitement, but I've never had a woman fall asleep on a date with me before."

"You should take that as a compliment. Think how comfortable I must be with you to nod off like that." I glanced at my watch and saw that, at least for me, it was late. I stood, shook the blanket, and then gathered it together. Jake walked me back to the house, kissed me good night, and then left.

When I walked in, Momma was reading

Carolyn Hart's latest. She loved the author for more reasons than her wonderful books. Even though we weren't related, we both still felt a kinship to her, a link through our last names. It was my dream to meet her one day, but I doubted life would ever bring her to April Springs.

"Have fun?" she asked as she put her finger on the page.

"It was glorious."

"Baked beans and all?" Momma asked with a definite twinkle in her eye.

"Yes, even then."

I fell asleep quickly, with Jake's last kiss still lingering on my lips.

# CHAPTER 19

"You're not going now, are you?" Emma asked me as I collected the last of the extra glazed donuts from the tray and moved them into a waiting box. It was just around four-thirty the next morning, and the day outside was still cloaked in darkness.

"I won't be long," I said. "You can handle the last few batches on your own." We'd made a double batch of yeast donuts, as I'd promised, and it was time to deliver the first run to the hospital. While I was there, I could check on George, too.

"Just don't stay past five-thirty, and we're fine," Emma said. She really didn't like it when I left Donut Hearts, especially when we were still preparing our offerings for the day, and I tried not to make a habit of it, but this just couldn't be helped.

"You can call your mother if you'd like." It was a safety net she didn't need, but if it made Emma happy, I wasn't about to say no.

"She's sleeping in," Emma said. "Go on, I'll be fine."

I was getting ready to grab the last box when my cell phone rang. "Hello?"

"Suzanne, it's Penny."

"Is something wrong? I was just on my way."

"Good. There's someone here who wants to talk to you."

I couldn't believe it. "George is awake?"

"He is, and cranky as can be. Any chance you have any old-fashioned donuts? He won't stop demanding one."

I laughed in relief. "Those are his favorites. I can bring them right now."

"I'm not sure he can have them yet, but go ahead and bring him one."

"I've got glazed for your crew, too," I said.

"Suzanne, I keep telling you, it's not necessary."

"But you won't turn them down, will you? I'm not even waiting for an answer. I'll see you in a few minutes."

I hung up, put my phone down on the counter, and collected a dozen of our old-fashioned donuts from the tray. Emma could see the broad smile on my face as she asked, "He's awake?"

"And causing trouble," I said. "He's demanding some of my donuts, so he must be getting better."

"Give him a kiss from me," she said.

"Will do."

I put the last box on top, and Emma got the door for me as I walked out to my Jeep. There was a little traffic on the Springs Drive, but it was easy driving all the way to the hospital. One nitwit behind me followed with their brights on, and from the look of it, the headlights hadn't been aligned in years. It was annoying, but I wasn't going to let it spoil my mood. George was awake, and better yet, alert.

When I got to the front desk, the guard must have been off somewhere else. I put a few glazed donuts on a napkin and left them for him, though. As far as I was concerned, the whole world could eat free today.

Penny met me at the ICU door. "I checked with his doctor. He can't have any donuts just yet."

"Save them for him, then," I said as I pulled the top box off. "The rest are for your lounge."

"You should have heard the doctors. They want in on these, too."

"Split them in half if you want," I said.

Penny smiled. "We might be able to spare

one box. Would you like to see him?"

"May I?"

"It's not strictly time yet, but there's not a nurse in this hospital who's going to say no to you today. Come on back."

I followed her through the glass doors, and past three curtained areas. At the fourth one, I found George.

He looked terrible. Both eyes were blackened, and there were tubes going in and out of him. A bandage was prominent over one brow, and his right leg was in a cast.

He never looked better to me.

When he saw me, his eyes brightened. "If you think I look bad, you should see the other guy."

I wanted to hug him, and I got close, but Penny put a hand on my shoulder. "He's a little sore right now."

"Come closer," George said, as though he wanted to whisper something in my ear. I did as he asked, but when I bent over, he didn't say a word, just inhaled as deeply as he could manage.

I pulled back and asked him, "What was that about?"

"They won't let me have any donuts, but I can still smell them on you."

I'd grown so accustomed to the smell that I hardly noticed it anymore. "Sorry, I didn't have time to shower and change."

"I love that scent. You should try to bottle it. You'll have your hands full of interested men."

"You're feeling better," I said, lightly touching his hand as if to be certain he was real and I wasn't dreaming.

"Believe it or not, I am." After a pause, he added, "I'm sorry, Suzanne."

"What do you possibly have to apologize for?"

"I can't remember anything," he said, the frustration showing on his face.

I'd forgotten about Penny, but she stepped in behind me as the monitor beat increased. "George, remember our talk? If you get upset, Suzanne has to go."

"I'm okay," he said, as his heart monitor soon attested.

"Don't worry about anything but getting better," I said.

"You're in danger," he answered. "The last thing I remember was talking to Cam Hamilton, there were some bright lights, and then I woke up here."

"Cam did this to you?"

The monitor started jumping again, and Penny said, "I'm sorry, but that's it. Suzanne has got to go."

"I'll behave myself," George promised again.

"Sorry, I don't believe you," she said with a smile.

"I'll come back later," I said as Penny walked me out.

"I told him he couldn't get too excited," she said. "Sorry about that."

"I understand. Did you tell the police about Cam?"

"I called them just before you got here. Chief Martin seemed very interested in having a talk with the mayor."

"I'll bet he is," I said. "Take care of him, Penny."

"I will," she replied. "And thanks again for the treats."

"Just remember to share," I said.

I started to walk outside, preoccupied with calling Jake, and I stepped off the curb wrong, twisting my left ankle and sending a shooting pain all the way up my leg. Great. Now I was having trouble just walking without injuring myself. I probably should have hobbled back inside and let Penny wrap it for me, but in truth I was too embarrassed to confess to my mishap. Instead, I made it to my Jeep and dialed Jake's number. My call went straight to his voice mail, so either he was still asleep, or he was on the case with Chief Martin. I couldn't do anything about either scenario, so I decided to go back to Donut Hearts where I could at least be productive while the case unfolded without me.

I was driving down a lonely stretch of road when the same high-beamed headlights I'd seen on my way to the hospital came up behind me again. What had George said about bright lights? Could that be Cam behind me? Had he hit George? It should be easy enough to check the mayor's car for possible evidence of an accident.

I had seen it earlier, though, and it had been fine.

Then I remembered picking up Cara Lassiter as she walked along the road. She'd claimed that her car had died, but what if it had sustained some damage from hitting George instead? Cara had been the closest person to Lester, but I'd discounted her as a suspect. Why? Because she'd been quick to give me other, more plausible reasons to suspect everyone but her. I had to give her credit for that; it had been very convincing. I couldn't think of a solid motive for her, other than her hatred of the victim, but I was sure Jake or the chief could turn that up.

A car's headlights coming the other way

lit Cara's face up for a split second before it passed us. I was right, for all the good it would do me. I dialed my boyfriend's number, and it again went straight to voice mail. "It's Suzanne. Cara killed Lester Moorefield. I'm sure of it."

I threw the telephone down on the passenger seat and focused on the road in front of me. I had to get out of this deserted stretch of highway. I hit the accelerator, hoping my Jeep had the power to elude her, but just as I did, my car started to die. It was all I could do to get it off the road before it quit entirely.

Cara stopped, as well. She'd clearly done something to my car, and now I was at her mercy, in the darkness, and in the middle of nowhere.

I searched the front of my Jeep for a weapon, but the only two things I could find were a lightweight flashlight and an unopened can of soda. When I looked behind me, I saw Cara step out in front of her headlights, a gun gleaming in her hands!

I had to get away, and I had to do it quickly. If I stayed where I was, I was going to die, and I knew it. My ankle was killing me, and I wasn't sure how fast I was going to be able to run, but I couldn't let the pain slow me down.

I grabbed my "weapons" and tore off into the nearby woods, nearly collapsing as I put weight on my ankle.

"Suzanne, where do you think you're going?" Cara asked as she raced to catch me. "Come back here."

"I don't think so," I yelled, using trees to lean against as I hurried away from that voice. I couldn't make much progress, and I wasn't getting far enough away from her quickly enough. I thought about waiting in ambush for her, but I couldn't be sure either one of my makeshift weapons would even slow her down. I tripped on a branch and went down just as she fired the first shot. I heard the bullet thunk into a tree nearby. Grabbing the branch, I wondered if I could use it as a weapon, or maybe even a crutch.

I had to leave the soda or the flashlight behind if I was going to carry that stick anywhere with me. I held my breath, let it out slowly, and then sat up as I threw the can at her with everything I had.

It missed by at least a yard.

Worse yet, now she knew exactly where I was.

In no time, Cara was standing over me. I hadn't gotten that far into the woods, and one of her cockeyed headlights still illuminated us.

"I'm glad that bullet didn't hit you," she said as she pointed the gun down at me. I'd managed to sit up, keeping one hand on the branch and the other on my light. "We need to talk."

"What is there to say? You killed Lester, and you tried to kill George when he found out."

"He's awake, then? How tough is that man? He should have been dead after I ran him down. If I'd had any idea how difficult it would be to kill him, I would have backed over him and finished him off properly. I guess I'll have to take care of that loose end after I deal with you."

"Leave him alone. He doesn't remember a thing," I said, hoping to save George's life, even if I couldn't save my own.

"Even if I believed you, I can't take the chance that it won't come back to him later."

"What did he find out that made you want to kill him?" I asked.

"George was digging around in my office at the radio station and he found a pair of hundred-dollar bills I'd left behind by accident. I must not have been too convincing when he asked me about them, because he told me we weren't finished. I spotted him walking to his car across the street, so I ran to mine and managed to run him down before he could get away." I saw a frown cross her face. "If George didn't tell you about our talk, how do you know I killed Lester?"

"There were lots of things," I said, stalling for time. Surely someone would drive by, spot our cars, and stop to help. That was one of the things I loved about living in the South. I knew for a fact that Cara's lights were blazing, and I'd left mine on in the Jeep. If I could stall her long enough, I might be able to survive this confrontation.

"Name them," she said, pointing the gun at me again.

When I was slow to answer, she nudged my bad ankle, and I cried out in pain. Cara just laughed. "I thought I saw you limping. I'm waiting, Suzanne. You'd better answer me, or it's going to get a lot worse for you real quick."

"You blamed everyone else, but you had to have had a reason to want him dead yourself." I thought about the things that could drive someone to murder, and believed that it all came down to sex, power, or money. I couldn't see the two of them having an affair, but the other two motives could each be true. "It was about money, and power," I said, trying to make my voice sound as confident as I could.

"Very good," she said.

I took a wild guess that suddenly made perfect sense. "Did you find the money he was hoarding from his embezzlement?"

She smiled. "As a matter of fact, I did. Wow, you're really good at this. He managed to keep a hundred grand without his investors or the cops getting it, but Lester didn't count on me. He was planning to run off, and he'd got it out of his safe-deposit box. I was looking for stamps in his desk drawer, if you can believe that, and found the money by accident. He caught me, and threatened to fire me if I said a word. I told him he couldn't, that I knew too much, and that he'd just given me a raise without knowing it."

"And he just stood there and took it?"

Cara's grin broadened, and she looked wicked in the diffused light. "He had no choice. I was the one with the power then. But I didn't trust him. It was clear Lester was scheming to figure out how to get rid of me, so I took care of him first." I glanced down, and saw that Cara was standing on the other end of the branch that had tripped me. Could I use that fact to my advantage? I had to keep her talking.

"How did you manage to strangle him?"

She laughed softly. "The fool was taping his farewell to April Springs when I came up behind him. I'd slipped some tranquilizers into his coffee earlier, and he kept nodding off. He was vulnerable sitting in that chair of his, and it was surprisingly easy to take care of him." She paused, as if remembering the crime, and then added, "I pushed him out the door in his chair and dumped the body where the police found it. Luck was with me that night. Not a soul was out. The station manager had brought a selection of your pastries that morning, so it was the perfect frame."

Was that a car on the road? We weren't close enough to know for sure, but I had to keep her talking. "So that's why you shoved an éclair down his throat."

"I thought it might be tough for you to explain after the fight you two had had. When you managed to convince the chief that you hadn't done it, it was time to start giving him more people to think about."

"You did something to my Jeep, didn't you?"

"With the Internet, it's amazing what you can pick up about disabling vehicles."

Another thought struck me. "What about your kids?" Cara had once confided in me

351

that her children were the reason she kept working for Lester.

"After we're finished here, I'm going to get them back from my ex-husband for good and we're starting over. Don't you see? I'm doing this all for them."

"Is anybody there?" a man's voice called out suddenly, closer than I could have imagined.

Cara swung her gun around toward him, and I knew that it was my only chance to act. I threw the flashlight at her as I yelled at the man to run, and then I grabbed the branch on the ground that she was still standing on. As I yanked it upward, it pulled Cara off her feet and sent her down to the ground, the gun flying out of her hand.

We both dove in the direction where it had fallen when a harsh beam of light penetrated the woods, and a man called out in a sharp voice, "Both of you, stop right there."

I'd never been so happy to hear Chief Martin's voice in my life.

# Homemade Pasta

When I first considered making my own pasta, I was a little intimidated, but in all honesty, it couldn't be easier. One warning, though; don't try making it on days that are overly humid. It honestly throws off the process. Some folks like to dry their home-made pasta, but I start a pot of water boiling as I'm cutting the pasta. No need for sauce, in my opinion. Some butter, freshly grated parmesan, and if you're in the mood, a little oregano, and you've got a meal.

## Ingredients
2 cups regular flour
1/4 teaspoon salt
2 eggs
1 tablespoon + cold water

## Directions
Sift the flour and salt together, and then place it in a bowl to make it easier to contain. Make a hollow in the flour (like a volcano) and add the eggs directly. Using a fork, beat the eggs into the flour, continuing to stir until it's all incorporated. Add a tablespoon of cold water, then mix it again. Don't overwork it; stop once the dough is no longer sticky to the touch. Flour a rolling pin, and roll the dough to 1/4 to 1/2

inch thick. I have a pasta machine that lets me thin the dough by rolling it through two rollers, but you can do it by hand, as well. Again, with a cutter or knife, separate the pasta into noodles, adding a little flour as needed.

Add the noodles to boiling water (slightly salted), and cook for three minutes, testing each thirty seconds afterward.

Makes enough for three to four people.

# CHAPTER 20

"Did she shoot you?" Chief Martin asked me as I struggled to stand. He'd cuffed her and retrieved her gun, and for once, Cara wasn't saying a word.

"No, I tripped," I said. I didn't clear up the fact that it had happened in the hospital parking lot instead of while getting away from a murderer. At least it sounded a little braver and a lot less clumsy.

"Here, let me help you," Jake said as he joined us.

"Have you got her?" the chief asked him as Jake took over.

"As much as anybody could," he said.

Chief Martin walked Cara back to his squad car, and Jake wrapped me in his arms, kissing me soundly. "I thought I'd lost you."

"I'm too tough for that," I said as I fought the very real urge to collapse.

"Sure you are," he said as he put an arm

around me. "How did she lure you out here in the first place?"

"She did something to my Jeep. It died on me as I was driving back to the shop from the hospital," I said. "I think she ruined it."

Jake said, "Don't sweat that. Whatever it is, we'll fix it. I'm just glad you're okay."

"Besides a little limp, I'm fine," I said.

As he helped me into his car, he asked, "When did you know it was Cara?"

"Three minutes before my Jeep died. I tried calling you," I said in my defense. "Your phone went straight to voice mail."

"I was helping the chief stake out Cam Hamilton's place," he admitted sheepishly. "We thought he was getting ready to run. Sorry about that."

"How could you have known?" I asked.

"I had a gut feeling that something was wrong, so I came looking for you at the hospital." He did a U-turn.

I asked, "Where are we going?"

"To the emergency room. You need to get that ankle looked at."

I decided I had to tell him the truth. "It didn't happen in the chase. I stepped off the curb when I left the hospital."

He laughed at my confession.

"It's not that funny," I said.

"I'm just happy it wasn't worse," he

answered. "Don't worry, I'm sure you'll be making donuts again in no time."

I glanced at my watch. It was nearly six, and I'd promised Emma that I would be back before we opened.

"I need your phone," I said.

"You don't need to call your mother. I took care of that as soon as I heard from the chief. She's meeting you at the hospital."

"I have to call Emma," I said.

"Hey, I'm sorry I'm late," I said when she answered the phone. I brought her up to date, and then remembered my promise to her dad. "Tell your father to meet me at the shop in half an hour, and I'll give him the full story. While you're doing that, ask your mom to come in and help. I'm afraid I won't be much good to you today."

"Are you okay?"

"I'm fine. Cara Lassiter is the killer, but I don't want to go into it right now. I'm going to have to tell this story enough times as it is, and you can listen while I bring your dad up to speed. Are we good?"

"As gold," she said.

Jake was still smiling at me as we drove up to the emergency room.

"Get that goofy grin off your face," I said. "I'm okay."

"I'm just amazed that with all that just

happened, your first priority is Donut Hearts. Suzanne, are you ever going to take a day off?"

"I don't know. Try to convince me."

"I'll see what I can do," he said as he pulled up to the curb.

An attendant met us with a wheelchair, and I was surprised when Momma wasn't close on his heels.

The surprise ended abruptly when I saw her talking with Chief Martin.

"What's all that about?" I asked Jake.

"I don't even want to guess," he said.

While I watched, Momma hugged the chief, something I never thought I would see in my lifetime. She looked at me guiltily and hurried over to where I was.

"Did you just hug him?" I asked.

"He saved your life."

"And that was his reward?" I asked with a grin.

"Actually, I've agreed to go out with him," she replied with a slight blush.

"I would hope I'm worth at least that much," I said.

"Suzanne, are you hurt?"

"Mostly just my pride," I answered. "My ankle got twisted."

"You're lucky," she said.

I patted Jake's hand, still on my shoulder.

"You don't have to tell me that."

After the X-rays showed nothing was broken, the doctor taped my ankle. Waiting for my discharge, I considered how our lives were about to change. It appeared that my mother was finally dating again, and Jake and I were getting closer with each passing day. Did that mean that the life my mother and I had carved out in the cottage was coming to an end? I was surprised to realize that I hoped it didn't happen too soon. There was a comfort there that I wasn't ready to give up, no matter how appealing the alternatives might be.

It was good to be so loved, and that was my richest possession.

Cara had murdered for money, but in the end, she'd have to pay for her crime, and lose her children forever.

I couldn't imagine any amount of money ever being worth that.

The next time I saw Jake, I was ready to reveal the surprise I'd planned for him.

"Did you mean what you said about your vacation time?" I asked.

"The offer's always open."

"Then I'm taking it," I said with a broad smile. "I can't get away for two weeks, but a weekend in Tennessee sounds lovely."

He looked shocked by the offer. "Do you

mean that? Can you afford to leave the donut shop?"

"Emma and her mother can handle it while I'm gone. The real question is, can I afford not to? If this case has taught me anything, it's that life gives you only so many chances at happiness, so you have to take every single one that comes your way."

"I'll make the reservations," he said.

As Jake talked to the innkeeper on the phone, I thought about how easy letting go was beginning to feel.

There was something else I looked forward to, as well.

I'd checked the lodge's Web site after Jake had mentioned the place, and I'd seen that they offered one of my favorites for breakfast every morning.

Fresh, homemade donuts.

We hope you have enjoyed this Large Print book. Other Thorndike, Wheeler, Kennebec, and Chivers Press Large Print books are available at your library or directly from the publishers.

For information about current and upcoming titles, please call or write, without obligation, to:

Publisher
Thorndike Press
10 Water St., Suite 310
Waterville, ME 04901
Tel. (800) 223-1244

or visit our Web site at:

http://gale.cengage.com/thorndike

OR

Chivers Large Print
published by AudioGO Ltd
St James House, The Square
Lower Bristol Road
Bath BA2 3SB
England
Tel. +44(0) 800 136919
email: info@audiogo.co.uk
www.audiogo.co.uk

All our Large Print titles are designed for easy reading, and all our books are made to last.